DO NOT DISTURB:
The Things Guests Do After Midnight

True Hotel Stories the Day Shift
Never Sees

DEDICATED

TO THOSE WHO STAYED AWAKE

SO OTHERS COULD SLEEP.

AND TO MY PARENTS,

Stavroula Kalogeropoulou

and

Eleftherios Pastrikos

AUTHOR'S NOTES

I didn't write this book to prove anything. I wrote it because the night has no voice. Those who work during the day see hotels. Those who work at night see people.

At night, there are no smiles for display. There is fear, desire, loneliness, power, mistakes, silence. And someone behind a desk who has to manage it all — alone.

Some of the stories in this book happened exactly as described. Some are condensed. Some are drawn from more than one real incident. And some could have happened on any night, in any hotel, in any city.

The people and events are presented as I experienced them, or as I remember them — not as a record, but as a narrative. Any resemblance to actual persons or situations is unintentional. First names are used for narrative purposes only.

What matters is that every story **is true in feeling**. And that is the only truth that counts.

TABLE OF CONTENTS

The Night Begins…

The night doesn't begin when the sun goes down. It begins when the last door closes behind the day manager. That's when the hotel changes. It breathes differently. The corridors grow longer. The shadows deepen. Voices lower — or slip out of control.

The lobby grows quiet, but it doesn't rest. Phones ring more clearly. Doors sound heavier. And every step matters more.

Somewhere in the middle of it all stands the night manager. Not to be remembered. But to make sure nothing bad is remembered.

He is not visible.

He is not the protagonist.

He doesn't appear in photographs. If he does his job right, his name will never be heard.

And yet, during those hours, he holds more than meets the eye. He holds people who cannot sleep. Situations balanced on a knife's edge. Decisions that must be made without time, without witnesses, without applause.

The night shift is not just a schedule.

It is a position.

It is a role.

It is a responsibility that cannot be written into a manual.

This book is not a guide.

It is not a handbook.

It is not a confession.

It is the nights as they truly are.

The nights you don't see in the morning meeting. The nights that don't fit into an incident report. The nights that, unless you live them, you never understand why someone leaves in the morning more tired than they should be.

The stories that follow are not a diary. They are moments. Nights. Situations that stayed upright because someone stayed awake.

If everything seems quiet, if in the morning there is nothing to explain, if no one remembers anything bad— then the night did its job.

And somewhere in the background, without anyone looking his way, the night manager simply… hands over the shift.

CHAPTER 1

The Shift That Never Ends

The first time I understood what the night truly means was when I found myself alone.

Not metaphorically. Literally. A large hotel. More than two hundred rooms. And behind the desk—me.

The shift always began calmly. Or at least, that's what you thought. Dim lighting in the lobby. A faint hum from the air conditioning. And that strange silence that is never really silence. It's waiting.

The first guests usually came down late. Some exhausted. Some irritated. Some already drunk— from the flight, the alcohol, or their lives.

And then it started.

Lines.
Passports.
Wristbands.
Glances that passed right through you, as if you were part of the furniture.

Some nights the line stretched all the way outside. Twenty meters of people who wanted their room **now**. Everyone believed their problem was the most important thing in the world. And I had to convince them that it was.

I asked for help.

They sent me a security guard. Not a hotel employee. Not someone from hospitality. Just a guy who knew the basics.

One night, close to midnight, I saw him pass through reception. He was tall. Solid. Nearly two meters. He was holding a tourist by the collar.

Literally.

He had lifted him slightly off the floor. He was pushing him toward the exit with kicks.

I stood still.

It wasn't fear. It was something worse. It was the moment I realized this wasn't hospitality.

No one was shouting.

No one reacted.

The other guests watched and pretended not to see.

That night I learned the first lesson of the job: the night manager is not a guard. He is a filter.

Between chaos and appearance. Between the human being and the system. And when a filter breaks, it doesn't show immediately. It shows later. In the stories that remain. The night went on.

And I stayed behind the desk, alone again. Back then, I didn't yet know when a shift truly ends. I thought it ended when you handed over the keys. When you shut down the computer. When you stepped outside and morning came.

I hadn't understood yet that some things don't leave with you in the morning. They just become quieter.

I didn't know then that this was only the beginning. That there would be nights that smelled of police. Nights when entire floors would flood. Nights when I would have to keep my hands down so they wouldn't rise.

The night manager's shift doesn't end when you clock out. It ends only when you stop remembering.

And that… almost never happens.

Night 1 – The First Check-In That Didn't Feel Right

The guest who arrived without a reservation... but with a lot of cash

There is an hour when the hotel changes its face. It's not midnight. It's a little after one.

That moment when the day is completely gone, but the night hasn't fully unraveled yet.

The hour when you think everything will pass quietly. You are almost always wrong.

I was alone at reception. The bellman had gone upstairs. The lobby was empty.

And then the door opened.

He didn't rush in. He didn't look around. He entered as if he already knew where he was. Tall. Dark coat. A clear look — not a tourist's.

"Good evening," he said.

"Good evening," I replied.

He approached the counter slowly.

"I need a room for tonight."

I checked the system. We were full.

"I'm sorry," I told him. "We have no availability."

He didn't frown. He didn't react.

He reached into the pocket of his coat. Pulled out a stack of banknotes. Placed them on the counter.

Not provocatively. The way you place keys.

"Check again."

He wasn't rude. That was the worst part.

I looked at the money. I looked at him.

Sometimes your job isn't to follow procedure. It's to listen to your instinct.

And mine told me something very clearly:

This check-in will not end well.

"I'll check again," I said.

Not because I had found a room. But because I needed time. To think. To decide. To choose a side. The night was just beginning.

Night 2 – The Hour You Start Paying Attention Differently

It was 02:40 when the door opened again.

This time he came in fast. Not anxious.

Decided.

You recognize that kind of step. It's not a tourist's. It belongs to someone who has already decided what he wants — you just have to give it to him.

"Check-in," he said.

No "good evening."

No "please."

He pushed his passport toward me.

I took it. Opened it. Looked at it.

The system showed what it had shown all night:

Full.

"We have no availability," I told him.

He didn't look at me.

He looked around.

The lobby was empty. No one behind him. No eyes to judge.

"But… I need to stay tonight," he said.

It wasn't a demand. It was a statement. Those are the most dangerous ones.

"I'm sorry," I repeated.

He leaned slightly forward.

Not threatening.

Conspiratorial.

"Do you know who I am?"

I didn't.

And I didn't want to.

"No," I replied.

He smiled.

Not nervously. Not sarcastically.

Like someone who had just realized he was talking to the wrong person.

"Okay," he said.

"Then tell me something."

He paused. Took a breath.

"Would you… let me in?"

It wasn't a question about a room. It was a question of character.

I looked at the screen again. Then at him.

There are moments when procedure says "no," and instinct screams "be careful."

"No," I said.

For the first time, the smile faded.

He didn't get angry. He didn't shout.

He did something worse. He straightened up. Picked up his passport. And said,

"We'll see each other again."

He turned.

Left.

The door closed softly behind him.

I was alone.

I didn't know why, but I felt I hadn't just said "no" to a check-in.

I had said "no" to something I wouldn't have been able to control. And at night, that matters.

Night 3 – Instinct Before Regulation

The problem with mistakes at night isn't that they happen. It's that they happen quietly.

The call came a little after three.

"Reception?"

The voice was low.

Female.

"I think… someone came into my room."

She wasn't shouting. She wasn't panicking. That worried me more.

"Are you sure?" I asked.

There was a pause.

Those pauses always say more than words.

"The door opened. Closed. And then… silence."

I asked for the room number. I told the bellman. We went up together. The corridor was empty. Quiet.
Too quiet.

I knocked.

Nothing.

"This is reception," I said.

"May we come in?"

The door opened slowly.

The woman stood a little farther back.
Dressed.
Awake.

"I didn't see a face," she said.

"The door just opened. Like someone had a key."

I checked the lock.

The system showed an opening ten minutes earlier.
With another card.

I looked at the bellman. He looked back at me.
These aren't simple mistakes. They're cracks.

"We'll change your cards," I told her.

"And no one else will be able to enter."

She nodded.

Not reassured.

Just… tired.

We went back down.

In the system, the card that opened her room belonged to another floor. Another side. Another story.

I went there.

Checked.

The guest was asleep.

Deeply.

He knew nothing.

Or at least, that's how it looked.

I returned to reception.

Wrote the incident report.

Clean.
Cold.

But inside, I knew:

Someone entered. Someone opened. Someone left.

And at night, that's enough to keep you from resting.

Night 4 – The Child Who Shouldn't Have Been Alone

There are nights that don't smell like alcohol. They don't have shouting. They don't have fights.

They have something heavier.

It was almost four when I saw him.

He didn't come down the elevator. He didn't enter through the door. He was already in the lobby.

Sitting on the couch.

Small.
Too small to be alone at that hour.

At first I thought he was waiting for someone. That's how children sit when they're bored: hands between their knees, eyes lowered.

"Hi," I said.

"Everything okay?"

He raised his head.

He didn't smile. He didn't flinch.

"Yes," he said.

The answer came too quickly. Like it was prepared.

"Who are you here with?" I asked.

He shrugged.

"My dad."

I checked the time.

04:02.

"Where is your dad?"

"Upstairs."

He didn't know the room.

He didn't know the floor.

"Do you want us to call him?"

He shook his head slightly.

"He told me to come down for a bit."

That's when I knew something didn't fit.

No parent tells a child to go down to the lobby alone at four in the morning. No parent who's okay.

"How old are you?" I asked.

"Ten."

I felt that tightening you can't see from the outside. But it freezes you inside.

I silently called the bellman over. Gestured for him to come closer.

"What's your dad's name?"

He told me.

A common name. Very common.

The system showed three guests with that name.

We went up.

The child in front.

Us behind.

On the fourth floor he stopped.

"Here."

The door was half open.

I knocked.

No answer.

I knocked again, harder.

"Reception."

Voices inside.

Not a child's.

A man opened abruptly.

The smell came out first.

Alcohol.
Something else.

"What's going on?" he said.

The child walked past him without a word.

"Your child was alone in the lobby," I said.

He looked at me. Then at the child.

"You went down?"

His voice wasn't worried. It was annoyed.

"I told him to wait."

I didn't respond.

It wasn't my job to make him a parent. It was my job to make sure that child didn't go down alone again.

"Please keep him inside," I said.

"And if you need anything, call."

He closed the door without answering.

We went back down.

The bellman didn't speak. Neither did I.

Some nights don't have an incident report.

But they stay.

Because nothing happened.

And that's what's most frightening.

Night 5 – When "Everything's Fine" Isn't an Answer

There are people who look at you and you know they're not seeing you for the first time. You just can't remember when you saw them.

It was a little after four. The hour when the body starts to weigh you down, but the mind has to stay awake by force. I was standing behind the desk when I heard footsteps.

I looked up.

He was alone. Well dressed.

No hurry.

He smiled before speaking.

"Good evening, Giannis."

My stomach tightened slightly.

Not from fear.

From instinct.

"Good evening," I replied. "Sorry… do we know each other?"

He shook his head.

"No. But I know you."

He didn't say it threateningly.

He said it naturally.

Like he was talking about the weather.

"You've been working here a while," he continued.

"Good at your job."

I didn't know what to say.

"Can I help you with something?"

He stepped a little closer to the counter. Not too close. Just enough.

"I just wanted to see who holds the night."

I glanced behind me instinctively. The lobby was empty.

"If you need anything, I'm here," I said.

He smiled again.

"I know."

He turned. Walked toward the elevator. He didn't go up. He went down. To the basement.

I stood still for a few seconds.

I checked the system.

There was no one under that name. There was no name at all.

I didn't write an incident report.

There was no reason. But from that night on, whenever someone called me by my first name without me remembering them—

I was a little more careful.

Because at night, the most dangerous thing isn't what you can see. It's what already knows you.

Night 6 – The Door That Closed Without Explanation

There are arrivals you forget. And there are arrivals that sit on your chest without you knowing why. It was just before five. The hour when the night is tired, but not ready to surrender.

The door opened again. A couple walked in. He in front. She half a step behind. They were both smiling. The same smile. As if they had practiced it.

"Good morning," he said.

It wasn't morning. But I didn't correct him.

"Good morning."

Check-in.

There was a reservation. Everything in order.

Passports.
Signatures.

The woman didn't speak at all.

She didn't look at me. She didn't look around the lobby. She looked only at the floor.

"First time in the city?" I asked out of habit.

"Yes," he answered immediately.

Too quickly.

I handed her the key.

On purpose.

Her fingers trembled slightly.

"The elevators are to the right," I said.

"We know," he replied.

I had never seen either of them before.

I watched them until they disappeared down the corridor. There was no reason to worry. No sign. And yet, I felt that weight.

At night, you learn to trust your instinct even when you can't explain it. Just before my shift ended, I passed by their floor.

Their door had a **Do Not Disturb** sign.

I didn't touch it.

Sometimes a smile is a defense.

And sometimes… it's a warning.

Night 7 – The Incident That Was Never Written

A cancellation at night doesn't always mean someone leaves. Sometimes it means the opposite. I saw it in the system a little after five.

A reservation had been automatically canceled. Room occupied. No checkout. No note.

These are the small things that pass during the day. At night, though… they light up.

I called the room.

"Reception, good morning."

No answer.

I called again.

Nothing.

I called the bellman.

"Let's take a walk."

We went up.

The corridor was quiet. The room door closed.

I knocked.

"Reception."

Silence.

I knocked again, harder.

"Reception. I need you to answer."

Movement inside. Footsteps. A chair scraping. The door opened a crack. An eye.

"What do you want?"

"Your reservation was canceled," I said.

"I need to confirm whether you're staying."

He opened the door a little more.

He was dressed. Didn't look like he was leaving.

"I'm staying," he said.

"You'll need to make a new reservation," I explained.

He looked at me like I had spoken another language.

"Who canceled it?"

"The system."

He smiled.

"Then let it do it again."

It wasn't a joke. It wasn't anger.

It was certainty.

"It doesn't work that way," I said.

The door opened fully.

Behind him, the room was… alive. Lights on. Suitcases open. As if no time had passed since check-in.

"I'm not going anywhere," he said quietly. "You understand?"

I did.

"You'll need to come down to reception," I said.

He looked at me for a few seconds. Then stepped aside.

"Fine."

We went down.

He made a new reservation. Paid. No comments.

As if nothing had happened.

When he left for the elevator, I checked the system.

The first reservation had been canceled from an IP outside the hotel.

Sometimes people don't leave when you cancel them. They stay to see how far you'll let them go.

Night 8 – The Man Who Didn't Exist in the System

Real VIPs never say they're VIPs. They just expect you to know.

It was almost six. The hour when the night starts to fray and mistakes come easier. The door opened and a man in a suit walked in. Not fresh. Worn for many hours.

Behind him, another man.

Silent. Like a shadow.

"Good morning," the first said.

"I have a reservation. VIP."

He said it like a title. Not information.

"Your name?" I asked.

He gave it. I typed it. I searched.

Nothing.

"Perhaps it's under another name?" I asked.

He smiled slightly.

"No. It's under *management*."

That's the word people use when there is nothing and they're waiting for you to bend.

"I'm sorry," I said. "I don't see any reservation."

The smile didn't leave. It just… froze.

"Maybe you should check again."

He didn't raise his voice. He didn't threaten.

He simply placed his hand on the counter.

And waited.

I looked at the second man.

He didn't look back.

"Without a reservation, I can't check you in," I said.

Silence.

Then he leaned slightly forward.

"Do you know who I work for?"

That question has no right answer. Only wrong choices.

"No," I said.

"And I don't need to."

He straightened.

For the first time, he looked annoyed.

"You'll hear about this."

"Probably," I replied.

He took a breath. Looked around.

The lobby was empty. No audience for a scene.

He turned.

Left.

The door closed.

I sat down for the first time all night.

I had no idea if I had done the right thing.

But I knew something else:

The people who "don't exist in the system" are the ones you need to watch most closely.

Night 9 – The Word "VIP" Without a Reservation

The police never arrive when you expect them. They arrive when you think the shift is over.

It was a little after six. The sky was starting to open. The lobby had that false dawn light.

And then there was noise outside.

Shouting.

Fast movement. A door opening hard.

Two police officers entered the lobby.

Behind them… him.

The same man from the night before.

The "VIP."

No suit now. No smile.

"This is him," he said, pointing at me.

The officers approached.

"Good morning," one of them said.

"Is there a problem?"

"He refused to check me in," the man said.

"I have the right to stay here."

I didn't react.

I didn't explain.

"Is there a reservation?" I asked calmly.

The officer turned to him.

"Sir?"

"It was supposed to be arranged," he said.

That sentence means nothing.

And everyone knows it.

"Without a reservation or payment, there is no obligation," the officer said.

The man looked at me.

For the first time, with clear anger.

"You think you won?"

I didn't answer.

"Sir," the officer said, "you need to leave the premises."

For a few seconds, I thought he wouldn't leave. That there would be a scene.

But in the end, he turned.

He gave me a look that wasn't a threat.

It was a promise.

The door closed.

The officers looked at me.

"Everything okay here?" one asked.

"Now it is," I replied.

They left.

The lobby emptied again.

I looked at the clock.

06:47.

In a few minutes, the morning shift would arrive. Everything would look normal.

But I knew:

Some check-ins don't end when the guest leaves. They end when you realize you did the right thing without knowing whether it will cost you.

Night 10 – The No That Was Said Calmly

The morning shift arrived the way it always does. Coffee in hand. Half-open eyes.

"Quiet night?" they asked.

I nodded.

It wasn't a lie. It just wasn't the whole truth. I handed over. Closed the drawer. Signed.

Everything as it should be.

I stepped outside.

The sun was a little higher. The street was waking up. People were going to work without knowing what had happened a few hours earlier.

I stood there for a moment. Didn't leave right away. I thought about the man who knew my name. The child in the lobby. The door that opened the wrong way. The "VIP" who didn't exist.

Not as incidents.

As warnings.

That's when I understood something that isn't written in any job description:

The night manager doesn't work only with people. He works with situations that don't show in the light. And if you make a mistake, it doesn't always show immediately.

It shows later.

In the stories that aren't told. In the looks that are avoided. In the names you remember without knowing why.

I walked home. Tired, but awake. Because that night I learned something simple and heavy:

This is not just a job. And anyone who can endure it never really leaves the night.

CHAPTER 2

"I Just Need a Key"… and Other Midnight Lies

The most dangerous sentence on the night shift isn't "we have a fire," or "call an ambulance."

The most dangerous sentence is this:

"I just need a key."

Because in this job, nothing is ever "just." And no one shows up at 02:47 in the morning for something simple—unless they are truly lost, or truly convinced they can take you for a fool.

I learned that quickly.

During the day, the receptionist hands out keys. At night, the night manager hands out… boundaries.

And boundaries, in a hotel, are not theory. They are the thin line between "good night" and "good morning, officer."

The First Lie: "I Was Just Here…"

It's always the same scenario.

A little before three. The lobby dimly lit. The TV on mute. The air making that soft *sssshh* sound that lulls you without you realizing it.

And you, behind the desk, holding the hotel in your hands like a glass filled to the brim. One sudden move, and it spills.

Then the door opens.

The guest walks in with the look of someone who has already decided that life, the universe, the weather are at fault— but definitely not him.

"Good evening. I need a key."

He says it the way someone asks for a glass of water.

"Of course, sir. Room number?"

Half a second of pause. That fraction of time where the truth looks for a costume.

"Uh… I'm in 417."

"Alright. Name on the room?"

"Well… I was just here. You know me."

Every time I hear *"you know me,"* I think how people believe hotels run on memory and emotion, not procedure.

"Sir, the system doesn't work on *you know me.* It works on a name and identification."

"Oh come on…" (and he smiles that half-smile that says *we're friends*)

"My wife is sleeping. Don't wake her up. Just give me a key."

"My wife is sleeping" is the second most common lie.

The first is *"I left my ID upstairs."*

"Of course. I'll just need to see your ID."

"I don't have it. It's in the room."

And right there, the night winks at you: *Welcome.*

You don't accuse him. You don't insult him. You don't embarrass him. You just hold the line.

"Sir, without identification I can't issue a key. I can escort you to the room and open it with you, so you can retrieve your documents."

That's usually where one of two things happens:

Either he suddenly remembers "Well… maybe I'm in 417… or was it 471?"

Or—

He disappears as fast as he appeared.

Both outcomes are a win.

Because at night, the goal isn't to prove you're right. It's to avoid the mistake that will follow you home.

The Second Lie: "I'm a Friend of the Owner"

There's another type of guest. He doesn't want a key. He wants power. He arrives at reception with the confidence of someone who already put on a VIP wristband—mentally.

"Good evening. I'm a friend of the owner."

"Good evening."

"I want to go up to Mr. —" (and he says a name like he's saying *open sesame*) "You don't need to ask."

This is the moment hospitality turns into a character test. Because hospitality ends the second someone tries to step on security.

"I'll need the guest himself to call us, sir. Or to come down and escort you."

"Seriously? You want me to wake him up now?"

"Yes."

That's it. One word.

But that word keeps rooms safe and keeps you standing.

The Third Lie: "They Told Me I Could"

My favorite one.

Responsibility by transfer.

"They told me I could have a late checkout."

"Who told you?"

"Well… your colleague."

"Which colleague?"

"I don't remember. One of them."

Inside that *one of them* hide a thousand things— from misunderstanding to a clean attempt to get something for free. You don't get angry here. You open the system. You check the logs. You read the notes.

And usually… there's nothing.

"Sir, there's no note regarding this.

I can confirm it with the morning manager."

That's when you see the switch flip in their face.

"Alright… never mind."

Never mind means *you caught me.*

And Then Comes the Call That Changes the Night

Those are routine. The small lies. But there are nights when a simple phone call throws you into a different level.

Back then, I was working at a central hotel in London. Where upselling was both art and mathematics.

The system was clear:

A guest books a lower category. You sell them a higher one. You earn commission. And they write it on a board. Not to praise you. Not to measure you but to motivate you.

The record belonged to an Italian, Simone. Duty manager, about to leave the hotel for another job.

His record was the kind we talked about like a legend.

£1,700 in upsales.

Everyone knew it wasn't easy to break— unless you ran into a guest who didn't ask *how much,* but said *okay.*

Two nights before Simone left, a guest came to reception.

Young.
Calm.
One of those people who look at you as if you're holding the remote control to the night.

"My father would like to speak to you."

He handed me the phone.

On the other end, the father. A voice full of certainty. Not a voice that asks. A voice that decides.

"I want a bigger room. Better than the one we booked. Do you have one?"

"Give me a moment to check the system."

I did what I always do: no promises, no rush, options only. In London, a *yes* you can't support turns into an incident by morning.

I found one category. A good one.

But the price difference wasn't small.

"There is availability. It's £220 more per night."

Silence.

That one second where you expect *that's too much, do something, I'm a regular guest.*

But none of that came.

"No problem. We'll take it. My son will pay.

" I hung up and felt something rare in night work: relief.

Not because of the commission. But because, for once, something was simple. The son checked into the new room. Took the keys. Said thank you. Went upstairs.

Then I opened the reservation.

Ten nights.

Ten.

I did the math in my head, afraid that saying it out loud would ruin it:

$220 \times 10 = 2200$.

I had broken Simone's record without chasing it. It had simply… happened.

I wrote it on the board.

And for the first time in my life, my hand wrote a number that felt illegal.

The Morning Simone Didn't Believe It

The next day, the FOM called me in.

"Well done."

The word landed heavy, like a rare coin.

Then he turned to Simone and smiled.

Mat said: "So now we won't have anything to remember you by, huh?"

Simone laughed indifferently— until he opened the reservation.

Ten nights. £220 per night.

His face changed like someone had pulled the rug from under him.

"Madonna…" he said.

Not out of jealousy, but of pure disbelief.

Do Not Disturb Is Not Always a Request

That same night, after the noise of the upsale faded and I was alone again, the hotel returned to its natural state: silence with traps.

There's a detail guests never see.

The night manager doesn't work only in the lobby. He works the corridors. The blind spots. The floors that creak. The doors that don't speak.

We call it a *floor walk*. I call it *the walk that teaches you not to smile too easily.*

You take the flashlight. The master key. The radio.

And you go.

At first it feels harmless. Carpets. Silence. A few snores. Ice clinking in a bucket somewhere. But the farther you go, the more you realize the hotel isn't sleeping.

It's just changing sounds.

And then you see the signs.

DO NOT DISTURB

On one door, it means exactly that. On another, it's a warning: *don't get close.* On a third, it's cover: *don't look.*

Do Not Disturb is like the smile at reception. It can be real. Or it can be defense.

You stand in front of the door and listen.

Not gossip. Security.

If you hear crying that stops abruptly, it's not always a fight. It can be fear. If you hear laughter that doesn't match the hour, it's not always a party. It can be something rushed.

And if you hear nothing at all— that's the strangest part. Because there are rooms that make noise. And there are rooms with too much quiet.

And when you see a door with *Do Not Disturb* hanging for three days straight, you don't think *what great guests, they don't ask for anything.*

You think:

Who doesn't want to be seen?

That's where the job stops being *hospitality* and becomes a filter. Again.

You don't knock without reason. You don't play sheriff. But you note it. You check logs. You verify housekeeping access. You ask in the morning, in a way that accuses no one. Because at night, the most dangerous thing isn't anger. It's *everything's fine* that doesn't sound fine. And *Do Not Disturb* often doesn't mean *do not disturb.*

It means:

Don't discover.

Because Keys Are Never Just Keys

That upsale was nice. A good story.

But it wasn't what made me a night manager.

Routine makes you a night manager. The lies. The people who test doors— literally and metaphorically.

Every *"I just need a key"* hides one of these:

- someone who forgot
- someone who's lying
- someone trying to enter where they shouldn't or
- someone panicking

And you have to tell them apart— without playing detective, without playing judge, without losing your humanity.

That's the hard part.

The easy part is getting angry. The easy part is saying *no* badly.

The hard part is saying *no* with a smile when you know that saying *yes* might make you write the next incident report.

That night, after the upsale, I returned to the desk.

Someone would come through that door again soon and say:

"I just need a key."

And I would do what I always do.

I would smile. I would ask for a name. I would ask for identification. I would hold the boundaries.

Because keys, in a hotel, open doors.

But at night…

they can also open mistakes.

And I wasn't there to open mistakes.

I was there to make sure none opened.

Night 11 – The Hour the Hotel Starts to Sound Different

It was one of those nights when nothing hinted at trouble. No shouting. No drunks. No complaints.

Just that heavy quiet that makes you glance at the lobby a little more often than you need to.

A little after three, the phone rang.

"Reception."

On the other end, a woman's voice.

Tight.

"Someone was in our bathroom."

She didn't say *came in*. She didn't say *I saw someone*.

She said *was*.

"Sorry?" I said.

"What do you mean?"

"Someone used the toilet."

I looked at my colleague. He looked back.

"I'm coming right up," I told her.

We went upstairs.

Mother and daughter were outside the room. Upset. Not hysterical. That's what worried me.

"Did you lock the door?" I asked.

"Yes. Always."

We went in.

The room was exactly the way they'd left it.

Beds made.

Bags in place.

But the bathroom… used.

Not carelessly. Not by mistake.

As if someone had walked in, done what they wanted, and left calmly.

"Did you see anyone?"

"No."

"Did you hear anything?"

"No."

I checked the corridor. Empty.

Cameras?
None on that floor.

I changed their keycards.

Explained what I could.

Offered a room move.

They didn't want it.

"We just want no one to come in again."

And then the thought came—the one you never want at night:

If it wasn't a mistake… then what was it?

There are cases where a card opens the wrong room.

Bad encoding. A glitch.

But this?

This didn't feel like a mistake.

Someone entered. Used the bathroom. Then… vanished.

Where did they go? With what card? To which room?

We never found out.

I went back down to the desk. Wrote the incident report.

Dry.
Professional.

But inside, I knew:

This wasn't one of the things you forget.

Because there was no explanation. And at night, the worst thing isn't anger or fear. It's the unanswered.

Night 12 – The Elevator That Wasn't in a Hurry

At 02:17 a.m., the elevator stopped.

Not abruptly. Not with a bang.

It simply… decided that this was far enough.

I was alone at reception, my coffee long past the point of usefulness, and the lobby quiet in that way that doesn't relax you— it warns you.

The phone rang once. Only once.

"Reception."

"Hello… we're inside the elevator."

The voice was calm. Too calm.

"Which elevator?"

"C."

Of course.

Elevator C never *broke.* Elevator C simply stopped when it wanted attention.

"We're coming," I said. "Stay calm."

I hung up and pressed the radio.

"Ramon."

The reply came immediately.

"Yes, boss."

Ramon had worked nights for years. Small, quiet, from the Philippines. He never raised his voice. Never panicked. When something went wrong, Ramon already knew where it was.

"Elevator C," I said. "We've got people inside."

"I'm coming," he said—like we were talking about coffee that went cold.

I took the stairs. Not out of fear—out of habit.

At that hour, you don't trust elevators.

On the third floor, the elevator doors were shut. Voices inside. Not panic. The voices of people trying to convince themselves everything is under control.

"I'm right outside," I said.

"Okay," a woman answered.

"It just… won't move."

"It doesn't have to," I said. "Just wait."

Ramon arrived beside me without a sound. Toolbox in hand like it was part of his arm.

"How many?" he asked.

"Two."

He nodded.

He opened the metal panel with calm, almost ritual movements. He wasn't rushing. He didn't look worried. As if he knew that if you push an elevator too hard, it pushes back.

"Talk to them," he murmured.

"We're here," I said. "My colleague is working the mechanism. In a few minutes, it'll open."

"Okay," the same voice said. "We can hear you."

The light flickered.

For half a second, no one spoke.

Ramon lifted his eyes.

"Don't worry," he said. "It always does that right before it opens."

I didn't know if he was talking to me or the elevator.

A metallic click.

The doors opened a little. Then more. The two guests stepped out slowly. They didn't run. They didn't speak right away. They looked like people who had just remembered what it feels like to stand normally.

"Thank you," the man said.

Ramon gave the smallest smile.

"You're welcome," he said. "Have a good night."

I stared at the empty elevator.

Its doors closed on their own.

Ramon packed his tools.

"It'll do it again," he said.

"When?" I asked.

He shrugged.

"When it needs to."

We went back to the lobby.

At 02:56 a.m., I wrote the report:

Subject: Elevator immobilization
Elevator: C
Guests: 2
Resolution: Manual release
Note: Monitor

I closed the file.

Ramon went back to work without another word.

A little later, I heard the familiar sound.

Ding.

I looked up.

Elevator C.

Lit.
Empty.
Ready.

Some nights, the hotel doesn't ask for explanations. It only asks you to stay awake.

Night 13 – The Kitchen Never Sleeps

At 01:43 a.m., the kitchen made a sound it shouldn't have made. Not an alarm. Not a scream.

A deep, metallic *thud*—like someone slammed a door angrily… from the inside.

I picked up the phone.

"Kitchen?"

"Yes, my friend… we have small problem," Alejandro said.

Alejandro's *small* was never truly small.

He was from Spain—polite, smiling, always spotless. His English came with that heavy Spanish accent that made every problem sound like something that would be fixed… just not right now.

“What problem?” I asked.

“The freezer door… is not agree with us anymore.”

I sighed and headed for the kitchen.

The kitchen at night is different. It doesn’t smell like food. It smells like effort. A little oil. A little soap. A little anxiety.

Alejandro stood in front of the freezer with his hands on his hips, as if arguing with an old friend.

Beside him was Papa-Nikos.

We called him that because he was the oldest—not because he was a priest, but because he had the eyes of someone who’d seen a lot and didn’t complain.

He’d left Greece in 2018. Not for dreams. For need. To work. To send money. To keep his family standing.

He stood with his hands behind his back and looked at the freezer the way you look at something that isn’t going to let you win.

“What happened?” I asked.

“It won’t close,” Papa-Nikos said. “And if it doesn’t close, it spoils. And if it spoils… we cry.”

Alejandro nodded gravely.

“Is emotional door,” he said. “Needs love.”

I bent down and looked.

A small box was caught in the corner.

Nothing serious.

Nothing that justified the tension.

"Take it out," I said.

Papa-Nikos removed it slowly, carefully, like he was lifting a mine.

The door closed.

Silence.

Alejandro stared at it suspiciously.

"No sound?" he asked.

"No sound," I said.

He grinned.

"She forgive us."

Papa-Nikos shook his head.

"Enjoy her," he told the freezer. "Until tomorrow."

We sat for a bit.

Alejandro made coffee.

Not good coffee— but the kind made at 2 a.m. to keep people upright.

"In Spain," he said, "we sleep now."

Papa-Nikos chuckled low.

"In Greece, at this hour… no work. We're at the bouzoukia."

None of us said why we were all here.

We didn't need to.

I returned to reception.

At 02:11 a.m., I wrote in the report:

Subject: Freezer door
Issue: Would not close
Resolution: Obstruction removed
Note: Operating normally

I closed the file.

The kitchen quieted down.

Not because it had no work— but because, for a moment, everything was in its place. And some nights, that's enough.

Night 14 – When the Noise Was a Person

"The key doesn't open."

He said it calmly. Too calmly for someone who had just been woken up. It was a little after four.

"Let me see it," I said.

He handed me the card.

It looked normal. Not old. Not damaged.

"Which room?"

"512."

The system showed something odd. Two active cards. One issued fifteen minutes ago.

"Who else is in the room?" I asked.

He shrugged.

"No one."

That was his first mistake.

"Then why are there two cards?"

He looked at me.

Not confused. Annoyed.

"I don't know," he said. "I just want to get in."

I made a new key. Encoded it. Handed it to him.

"If it still won't open, we'll go up together."

He didn't answer.

Ten minutes later—back at the desk.

"It still won't open."

I looked at him.

"Let's go."

On the floor, he stayed half a step behind me. Like he didn't want to be seen. I opened the door. The room wasn't empty.

A woman was sitting on the bed. Wrapped in a sheet. With the look of someone who had just realized something had gone very wrong.

"Who is he?" she asked.

The man said nothing.

"Ma'am," I said calmly, "are you registered to this room?"

"No," she said.

"I just got here."

I looked at him.

"Sir, you need to come with me."

He didn't react. In the elevator, the silence was heavy.

"The room is under your name?"

"No."

"Then how did you get a key?"

He didn't answer.

At reception, I explained it simply:

No reservation. No identification. No access.

He left without shouting.

Without threats.

The woman changed rooms. Apologized without being at fault. When I was alone again, I thought:

Some people never lie. They just leave gaps. And at night, gaps are more dangerous than lies.

Night 15 – Everyone Awake, No One Normal

At 02:04 a.m., we were all there.

A rare thing. Like a full moon in the rain.

Me at reception. Ramon beside me, leaning on the counter as if he were an extension of the furniture.

Alejandro had come down "for one minute." Papa-Nikos had stepped out of the kitchen "to see what's going on."

No one knew what was going on.

But all of us were sure something would.

Ramon watched the camera screen.

"Lobby very quiet," he said.

Alejandro leaned forward.

"Too quiet," he said seriously. "This is movie moment."

Papa-Nikos snorted.

"Easy there, Hollywood. It's two in the morning."

Alejandro looked at him, genuinely puzzled.

"Papa Nikos… why you always angry but smiling same time?"

Papa-Nikos turned slowly.

"Experience."

Ramon smiled without lifting his eyes.

"Papa Nikos angry default setting."

"You talk less," Papa-Nikos said to him. "You always smile. Suspicious."

"If I stop smiling," Ramon said, "problems start."

Silence.

Alejandro broke it.

"Guys… question."

We all looked at him.

"If guest ask for extra pillow at 3 a.m… is emergency?"

Papa-Nikos laughed.

"If he's Greek, yes. If he's English, he'll be too embarrassed to ask."

Ramon nodded.

"English guest say sorry before problem. Filipino say sorry after problem. Greek never say sorry."

"What are you talking about?" Papa-Nikos said.

"Fact," Ramon replied calmly.

Alejandro raised both hands.

"In Spain we say sorry… and then we do again."

We laughed.

For a moment, we forgot we were working.

Then we heard the familiar *ding* of the front door.

We all froze.

Ramon looked at the screen.

"Guest incoming."

Papa-Nikos straightened his back.

"Alright," he said. "Work."

Alejandro whispered:

"Showtime."

A man walked in wearing pajamas and socks.

"Sorry to bother," he said.

Ramon smiled instantly.

"No bother, sir."

"I just… can't sleep."

Papa-Nikos looked at him with understanding.

"Neither can we," he muttered.

Alejandro leaned in.

"Coffee?" he asked.

"At this hour?" the guest said.

Papa-Nikos shook his head.

"In Greece, at this hour… you're just getting started."

The guest smiled awkwardly.

"Just a glass of water."

Ramon handed it to him before he finished the sentence.

"Here you go."

The man thanked us and left.

The door closed.

Silence again.

Alejandro broke it.

"Nice team."

Ramon nodded.

"Good night team."

Papa-Nikos put on his jacket.

"Alright, I'm going out for a cigarette. If you hear a commotion… don't come."

"Why?" I asked.

"Because it'll be the fridge."

We laughed.

I was alone at reception again.

Some nights nothing happens. And yet, those are the ones you remember most.

Night 16 – The Key

She didn't come to ask for a key. That was the strange part. It was close to four when I saw her standing a little away from the desk. Not coming closer. Not leaving. Just standing there— as if she needed permission to speak.

"Good evening," I said.

She lifted her head sharply, like I'd caught her doing something she shouldn't.

"Good evening…" she whispered.

Nothing else.

"Can I help you?"

She nodded yes, but her feet didn't move.

"I can't find my room," she finally said.

"Do you have your key?"

She reached into her bag. Searched. Searched again.

"I think… I lost it."

She didn't look like the kind who "loses it" on purpose.

She looked lost in general.

"Name on the room?" I asked.

She told me.

It was there.

"ID?" I asked.

She pulled out her wallet immediately.

No reaction.

No tension.

I looked at her. A little longer than usual.

"I'll walk you up," I said.

She didn't protest. She just exhaled, as if a weight had left her.

In the corridor she walked half a step behind me.

As if she was afraid to go first.

"Are you alone?" I asked.

"Yes."

"Do you want me to change the keycards?"

"Yes," she said quickly.

"Please."

I opened the door.

The room was dark. Untouched.

She went inside without speaking.

"Everything okay now?" I asked.

She turned to me.

"Yes," she said. "Thank you for… not asking more."

I nodded.

"Rest well."

I went back down to the lobby.

I didn't write an incident report. There was no reason. But I knew one thing:

Some people never ask for a key. They're just asking to feel safe enough to enter somewhere. And sometimes, that's the hardest request of the night.

Night 17 – A Presence Without Permission

Some guests lie. And some guests don't even know what they're saying. It was around 3:30 when he came into the lobby. He walked slowly.

Not drunk. Not tired.

Lost.

He stopped at the desk and looked at me like he was trying to remember me.

"Good evening," he said.

"Can you give me my key?"

"Of course," I said. "Name on the room?"

He looked at me again— as if he expected the question to change.

"My… name?"

I nodded.

"Yes."

Silence.

"Sorry… which hotel am I in?"

In that moment, the whole night shifted gears.

"You're at the —," I said calmly.

"Are you feeling okay?"

He shook his head.

"No, no… I just…"

"I was somewhere else before."

There was no smell of alcohol. No panic. Just a clean blank.

"Do you have any ID on you?" I asked.

He took out his wallet.

Handed me his ID.

His name was in the system. A room existed. Two nights.

"I can walk you up," I said.

"Yes… better," he murmured.

In the corridor, he moved slowly, as if counting his steps.

"Does this happen often?" I asked.

"No…"
"At least I think it doesn't."

He entered the room. Looked around.

"Yes… this is it."

He sat on the bed without taking off his shoes.

"If you need anything, call," I said.

"Thank you…"

"And sorry."

I went back down.

I added a note in the system. Not an incident. An observation. Because some nights you're not guarding doors. You're guarding people from themselves.

Night 18 – The Right Key

She didn't shout. She didn't cry.

That worried me more.

It was a little after four when she approached the desk. A woman around forty. Hair done. With that look that tries to stay upright while everything inside is collapsing.

"Excuse me…" she said.

"Could I have a second key?"

"Of course," I replied.

"Name on the room?"

She told me.

It was there. Room occupied. Two guests.

"ID?" I asked.

She didn't object.

She just hesitated.

"It's… upstairs," she said.

"In the room."

She looked up.

"I can't go up there alone right now."

It wasn't a complaint.

It was a statement.

"Would you like me to walk you up?" I asked.

She nodded yes—too quickly.

In the elevator, she didn't speak.

Neither did I.

On the floor, before we reached the door, she stopped.

"If he's angry…" she said quietly.

"Just—stay a little behind me."

I didn't ask *who.*

I didn't ask *why.*

I opened the door first.

The room was dark. Only the bedside lamp was on. A man sat on the bed, his back to us.

He turned slowly.

"What is this?" he said.

"Good evening," I said.

"I'm walking your wife up."

He didn't answer.

The woman went inside. Straight to the bathroom. Closed the door.

The man looked at me.

"You don't need to be here."

"I know," I said.

"I'll be leaving in a moment."

I stood up slowly.

When the woman came out, I handed her the second key.

"If you need anything," I said,

"at any hour."

She nodded. Her eyes shone, but not a single tear fell.

I went back down.

I didn't write an incident. I didn't write a note. Because it wasn't a hotel issue. It was a moment. And some nights, the right key doesn't open doors.

It opens time.

Night 19 – When You Don't Lose the Key, You Lose Your Direction

Sometimes the key isn't asked for. It's implied. It was close to 4:30 when I heard the elevator open.

Not footsteps.

Dragging.

A man came out.

Middle-aged.
Barefoot.
Wearing only pajama pants.

In his hands he held… nothing.

He stopped in front of the desk and looked at me like he had woken up in the wrong life.

"Good evening," I said.

No answer.

"Can I help you?"

He took a breath.

"I can't find my room."

Not the key.

The room.

"What's your name?" I asked.

He told me.

It was in the system.

"Do you have your key?"

He looked at his hands as if expecting it to appear.

"No."

"Where did you last see it?"

He shrugged.

"I don't remember."

There was no panicked confusion.

Just emptiness.

"I'll walk you up," I said.

He nodded.

In the corridor, he walked slowly, like he was afraid that if he rushed, something would break.

He stopped in front of a door.

"Here," he said.

I tried the card.

Nothing.

Again.

Nothing.

"This isn't it," I said.

He looked at me with the expression people get when they realize they're completely lost.

"Then where is it?"

"We'll find it," I said.

Two doors down, I opened the right one.

He went in without speaking. Sat on the bed.

"Thank you," he said after a moment. "I thought that… never mind."

"Do you want me to change the keycards?" I asked.

"Yes… that would be good."

I handed him the new key.

He held it with both hands, as if it were fragile.

I went back down to the lobby.

I thought about how easy it is to get lost in a hotel.

Not because it's big.

But because at night, if you get lost inside yourself, no key finds you quickly.

CHAPTER 3

"Do Not Disturb" Is Only a Suggestion

There's a moment—always after one—when the hotel looks quiet.

It's the most dangerous moment.

The lobby lights are lowered. The elevator goes up and down less often. Most people believe everything is over.

But the night doesn't end.

It just changes character.

That's when the checks begin.

The so-called **floor walk**.

It's not a stroll. It's not a routine formality. It's like walking through a living organism that sleeps with one eye open.

You keep the keys in your hand. The radio turned down. And you walk.

Corridors at night are never empty.

Even when you don't see anyone, you hear.

The sounds behind the doors

Sometimes it's fighting. At first, whispers. Then tension. Then silence. Two people who walked into the same room to be saved, and now are trying not to fall apart. Sometimes it's moaning. *Ah... ah...* louder than it should be. Like an unofficial hallway competition—especially on Friday and Saturday nights.

And then... the snoring. So loud it goes through walls. Two or three rooms down. That's when you learn something no training ever tells you:

Hotels are never as soundproof as we pretend.

The Flood on the Fourth Floor

That night, on the fourth floor, I didn't hear it first.

I felt it.

Cold in my shoes.

I looked down.

Water.

Not a little.

Three centimeters deep. Half the floor flooded.

I called for help. We started opening doors.

Six rooms were already taking water.

We found it at the end of the corridor.

A door half open.

We went in.

The bathtub filled to the top. The water still running.

And the guest…

asleep.

A Chinese gentleman. Calm. Still. As if nothing had happened.

We woke him.

He shot upright. Apologized again and again.

He couldn't believe what he'd done.

He paid a large part of the damages, and left the next day embarrassed. Later I learned that for some people this isn't unusual. They fill the tub. They lie down. And time stops.

But the night never does.

"Come in…"

And then there are the moments no one prepares you for.

On a floor walk, two girls opened their door.

Towels wrapped around them.

"Come in," they said.

"We'll have a good time."

I looked at them.

I smiled awkwardly.

"I'm sorry. I can't."

Did I do the right thing?

I don't know.

Maybe I missed the story of my life.

Maybe I simply did my job.

And at night, that matters.

Because "Do Not Disturb" Never Means What It Says

People think the little sign on the door is a boundary.

It isn't.

It's a suggestion. A wish.

At night:

- doors open,
- boundaries blur,
- and privacy becomes negotiable.

And you're there not to judge.

But to prevent.

Because every sound you ignore, every door you don't pay attention to, can become the incident everyone talks about in the morning.

I went back to reception. Sat behind the desk. The corridors kept breathing. And I kept listening. Because a night manager doesn't always see.

But he hears everything. And some things… you'd better be the first to hear.

Night 20 – The First Walk

At 01:18 a.m., Alejandro looked at Nikos and handed him the keys.

Not like a ceremony. Like a responsibility.

"Floor walk," he said in that heavy Spanish accent. "Not walking for fun. Walking for survival."

Nikos smiled awkwardly. He was new— not only to the shift, but to the country, the job, everything.

His parents had come from Albania to Greece for a fresh start. Now he had left Greece to find his own.

"What do we look for?" he asked.

Alejandro opened the door to the second floor.

"We don't look," he said. "We listen. Like doctors. Or criminals."

The corridor was quiet. Too quiet.

"Is that good?" Nikos asked.

Alejandro shook his head.

"Too quiet is suspicious. Like when Spaniard not talking."

They walked slowly. The keys made a small metallic sound.

Nikos moved to put them in his pocket.

"No," Alejandro stopped him.

"If something happen, you want sound. Sound is warning."

A little farther down—whispers.

Nikos slowed.

"Fight?" he whispered.

Alejandro tilted his head.

"Pre-fight. Like warm-up."

The voices rose a little. Then fell.

"We don't go?" Nikos asked.

"Not yet," Alejandro said.

"If we go too early, they hate us. If we go late, they hate us more."

They kept moving.

Moaning. Not subtle at all.

Nikos blushed.

"Uh… that…"

Alejandro smiled.

"Weekend," he said.

"People remember they are alive."

Farther down—snoring. Loud.

"That one will be a complaint," Nikos said.

"Yes," Alejandro replied.

"From someone who snore too, but less."

They turned the corner.

Nikos felt something cold.

He stopped.

"Water…"

Alejandro sighed.

"Ah. Bath lovers."

The water led to a half-open door. Light. A bathtub filled to the brim.

The guest was asleep.

Nikos whispered, "And now?"

Alejandro stepped closer.

"Now we become alarm clock," he said.

They woke him gently. The man startled awake, apologized, almost bowed.

Alejandro calmed him.

"No problem, my friend. Hotel still standing."

They stepped back out.

Nikos took a deep breath.

"If we'd been late…"

"Fourth floor swimming pool," Alejandro said. "Very exclusive."

They returned to reception.

Nikos sat behind the desk differently than he'd stood up.

"'Do Not Disturb'…" he said.

Alejandro smiled.

"Is suggestion," he said.

"Like speed limit."

Nikos laughed.

"And the walk?"

Alejandro winked.

"Is when hotel pretend to sleep. And we pretend too."

Nikos nodded. He wasn't just new anymore. He was part of the night. And the night… doesn't forget.

Night 21 – Do Not Disturb

The *Do Not Disturb* sign always hangs on the outside.

The argument always happens inside. It was a little after two when the first call came.

"Reception."
"There's something going on in the next room. They're shouting."

The voice on the other end wasn't angry. It was tired. The kind that doesn't want trouble, but can't take it anymore.

"Thank you," I said. "I'll check it."

I took the groom and we went up.

The corridor was quiet.

Too quiet for what had come before.

We stood outside the door.

And then we heard it.

Not clear voices. Not words. Sounds.

Something between anger and crying. A word cut in half. A *no* said too late.

I knocked.

"Reception."

Silence.

I knocked again.

"Reception. Please open."

Movement inside. Someone walking fast. Something falling.

The door opened slightly

A woman.

Red eyes. Messy hair.

"Is everything okay?" I asked.

Behind her, a man. Bare from the waist up.

His expression angry—but not toward us.

"Yes," she said quickly.

"We're just… talking a bit loudly."

I didn't believe her.

I didn't need to.

"There's been a disturbance reported from nearby rooms," I said.

"We'll need to keep the noise down."

The man laughed sarcastically.

"We're in a hotel. Not a monastery."

I looked at him.

"True," I said.

"But we're also next to other people."

The woman lowered her eyes.

"Sorry," she said.

"It won't happen again."

She closed the door.

We went back down.

Ten minutes later, the second call.

"It's worse now."

I went back up alone.

I knocked.

"Reception."

No answer.

I knocked harder.

"Reception. Open the door."

This time, he opened it.

"What do you want now?"

"This needs to stop now," I said.

"Otherwise we'll involve security."

He looked at me.

For the first time, not angry.

Afraid.

"There's no need…"

"There is," I said.

He glanced behind him.

The woman was sitting on the bed. Silent.

"Close the door. Get some rest," I said.

"And if you need anything… call."

It wasn't a threat.

It was a boundary.

The door closed. Nothing else was heard from that room that night. But I knew something.

Do Not Disturb protects sleep.

Not relationships.

And at night, a night manager doesn't knock on doors for noise. He knocks to see whether what's behind them is just an argument or something that shouldn't continue. That sign doesn't protect people. It protects the image.

And the night manager exists for the moments when you have to look past the door and understand whether what's behind it is just noise or something that must be stopped.

No incident report was written that night.

But something else was. That at night, the most dangerous thing isn't the argument.

Night 22 – The Day Shift Who Couldn't Sleep

The transition from day shift to night shift isn't a change of schedule.

It's a change of personality.

During the day, everything has rules.

At night, rules have exceptions.

That night my assistants were Alejandro from Spain and Michele from Italy.

Michele was one of those good guys you never want to disappoint. Polite. Well-groomed. A little gay— not as a judgment, just that in the looseness of the night he made awkward gestures— a bit insecure, prone to small mistakes.

During the day, he was perfect.

At night, he kept asking whether things he'd done correctly ten times already were still correct.

"Boss…"
"Yes, Michele."

"The charge in the PMS… is it right?"
"Yes."
"Are you sure?"
"Yes."
"Because the system didn't tell me anything…"
"If the system talked," I said, "we'd all have quit."

Alejandro smiled behind the counter.

"Relax, amigo," he said in his heavy Spanish accent.
"If something wrong, hotel shout. Hotel always shout."

Michele did not relax.

At 01:40 a.m., we started the floor walk.

"We walk and listen," I told him.

"We don't look."

"What do you mean?" he asked.

Alejandro answered first.

"Doors talk at night."

Second floor: whispers.

Third floor: moaning with no intention of

discretion.

Fourth floor: snoring like an old bus engine.

Michele blushed.

"Should we… intervene?" he whispered.

"No," I said.

"Just remember: *Do Not Disturb* is a suggestion. Not a law."

I turned to see if he understood.

He didn't.

But he was recording it.

Back at reception, Michele stood behind the desk straighter than he had in the morning.

At one point, he passed very close to me.

Too close.

He brushed against me low, almost by accident.

He looked at me and smiled.

"Oooh boss… nice snake you have."

I froze for half a second.

Looked at him.

"Respect Malaka*," I said in English and in Greek.

Malaka (μαλάκας | Greek slang)
*A uniquely Greek word with **no single English equivalent**. Literally, it's an insult. Culturally, it's everything else.*
*Malaka can mean: friend, idiot, bro, jerk, mate, you absolute legend, you absolute disaster. Sometimes all **in the same sentence**. Its meaning depends entirely on: tone of voice, timing, relationship, and how late at night it is*
Said with a smile, it means "my guy."
Said with anger, it means "don't push your luck."
Said quietly at 03:00 a.m., it usually means "I can't believe this is my life."
*In Greece, malaka is not just a word. It's a social tool. A pressure valve. A warning. And occasionally, a term of affection. Most foreigners learn it on day one. Very few ever learn when **not** to use it.*

Alejandro leaned forward, laughing.

"What snake?"

"Don't ask," I said. "Night shift incident."

Michele turned red to the ears.

"Sorry! Sorry! I joke!"

"Relax," I said. "Just… choose better timing."

He laughed.

For the first time all night, he didn't ask anything.

Michele left in the morning exhausted. But smiling. He hadn't learned all the secrets of the night yet. But he had understood the basic one:

At night, you don't need to do everything right. You just need to know when not to disturb and when to keep your distance.

Even from snakes.

Night 23 – The Guest in the Corridor

The groom didn't speak right away. He looked at me first.

"Boss… we've got a guest upstairs."

"Upstairs where?"

"Fourth floor. In the corridor."

We went up together. Not running. Running at night doesn't help—it gives you away.

I saw him before we reached him.

Lying right outside his room door.

On his side. One arm stretched out.

His wallet open next to him, as if he'd tried to take something out and didn't make it.

"Sir?" I said loudly.

"Can you hear me?"

Nothing.

I bent down. Touched his shoulder.

His body was heavy.

Not relaxed. Not like sleep.

"Open the room," I told the groom.

The card opened with that sound that feels too loud at three in the morning.

We went in.

No time wasted.

We grabbed him by arms and legs and put him on the bed.

I turned his head to the side. That's when he started breathing. Heavy. Uneven. Like something was pulling him back.

"Call an ambulance," I said.

I stayed next to him.

Not as a manager.

As a human who didn't know whether in two minutes he'd be writing a report or closing someone's eyes.

The paramedics arrived.

They checked him.

They took him.

The corridor emptied again.

I picked up his wallet.

Closed it.

Left it in the room.

That night I understood something no training ever tells you: A night manager isn't only there for the living. He's also there for those who almost didn't make it.

Night 24 – Pleasure Took Him

The call came just before three. It didn't ring loudly. It didn't ring insistently. It rang sharp.

"Reception…"

For half a second, I heard nothing.

Then the voice came.

"My husband… he's not breathing well. Something is wrong."

She wasn't screaming.

That's what made me stand up immediately.

"I'm coming now," I said. "Stay on the line."

I hung up.

Called the groom.

We went up.

No one spoke in the elevator.

The room was dark.

The door open.

I went in first.

The man was lying on the bed.

Naked.

His body rigid.

His face had that color you never forget.

Not blue. Not white.

Something in between. Something wrong.

On the bedside table were pills. Blue. From a known brand.

Not scattered.

Placed neatly.

And that detail that drills into your mind whether you want it to or not:

The body had reacted, while the man was already gone. The woman stood beside the bed.

Russian.

Her gaze empty.

"When?" I asked.

"I don't know," she said.

And then nothing.

We started CPR.

Not because we believed.

Because we had to.

I called the ambulance. Gave details. Again and again.

Thirty minutes.

When they arrived, they already knew.

They understood before touching him.

"Time of death…" one of them said quietly.

I stepped back.

There was nothing else to do.

The woman sat on the chair.

She didn't ask anything.

The next day, she didn't leave.

She stayed.

And the second.

And the third.

We didn't charge her.

No one even considered it.

On the third day, a private jet arrived from Russia.

It was his wife.

Not for her.

For him.

She took his personal belongings.

Signed.

Thanked us.

The two women never met.

The woman who was there and the wife who came after.

When the room was finally empty, I went in alone.

The bed made. The curtains open. Nothing looked out of place. And yet, everything was there.

That night I learned something not written in any SOP: That in hotels, people don't come only to sleep.

Some come to finish. And the night manager is the only one who sees it first.

CHAPTER 4

The Call Button from Hell

There's a button at reception that doesn't look dangerous.

Small.
Plastic.
A little red light next to it.

It doesn't say *Danger*. It doesn't say *Panic*.

It just says: **Call.**

And yet, that button has ruined more nights than I can count. Because it never rings for something reasonable. It always rings at the wrong moment. And almost never for something that couldn't wait until morning.

02:47 a.m.

I don't know why, but it's always 02:47.

Not 02:30.

Not 03:00.

02:47.

The hour your body is starting to give up but your mind is still fighting to stay upright.

And then—

Ding.

The red light flashes. The button stares at you.

I pick up the handset.

"Reception, good evening."

Silence.

"Hello… can you hear me?"

"Yes, I can hear you."

"I just wanted to ask…"

This is where you always hold your breath.

"…what time does breakfast start?"

I look at the clock.

02:47.

"From 7:00 a.m., sir."

"Oh, great. Thank you."

Click.

I sit back in my chair and think:

If breakfast started at three, you'd already be there.

"Sorry to bother you…"

There is no more dangerous phrase than that one.

Because anyone who says *sorry to bother you* knows exactly that they're bothering you.

"Sorry to bother you, but…"

"Yes?"

"The Wi-Fi isn't working."

"One moment, I'll check—"

"No, no, no, you don't need to check. I just wanted to tell you."

Silence.

"Would you like me to do something about it, sir?"

"No, I just wanted you to know."

Click.

That call had no purpose.

It had a need.

Some people simply can't handle the silence of the night.

So the hotel becomes a confessional.

The Button That Rings Just to Ring

And then there are the others.

"Reception, good evening."

"Yes, I'm in 312. The room next door is making noise."

"What kind of noise, sir?"

"How do I put it… he's… living."

I go up.

I knock politely.

A guy opens with a grin from ear to ear.

"Problem?"

"Noise complaint."

"Oh, sorry. We'll keep it down."

I go back down.

Two minutes later—

Ding.

"It's me again. Now it's worse."

I go back up.

This time, no one opens.

I knock harder.

"Reception."

Nothing.

I go back down.

Two minutes later—

Ding.

"You didn't do anything."

That's when you understand something:

They don't want a solution.

They want an ally.

They want to feel like someone is on their side against the night.

"Can you bring me…"

The button doesn't ring only for complaints.

It rings for requests that don't exist in any manual.

"Can you bring me a charger?"
"Unfortunately not, sir."
"At least a cable?"
"No."
"A different pillow."
"Of course."
"And a glass."
"Certainly."
"And some ice."
"I'll do my best."
"And…" (pause) "sorry, do you also have a painkiller?"

That's where you stop.

"Sir, we're not allowed."

"Come on. Just a Depon."

And again— the smile. the boundary.

The Call You Never Want

But sometimes…

the button rings for the right reason.

"Reception!"
"Yes—tell me."
"My husband won't wake up."

The voice changes.

No irritation. No demands.

Fear.

That's when you don't think SOP.

You think human.

"I'm coming now. I'm calling an ambulance."

You run upstairs.

And then you understand why you spent the whole night keeping yourself calm. Because this is the real test. Everything else was rehearsal.

Because the Button Never Truly Goes Quiet

Until sunrise, the button will ring again. For something trivial. Something absurd. Or something you'll remember for years. And every time, you'll answer with the same voice:

"Reception, good evening."

Because at night, it doesn't matter what wakes you up.

It matters how you respond.

And the night manager always responds.

Even when inside…

he'd give anything for a little silence.

Night 25 – The Button Never Lets All of Us Go

Saturday night.

338 rooms.

338 occupied.

The hotel wasn't asleep.

It was pretending.

Two venues had closed at midnight. Which meant:

- extra cleaning,
- drunk returns,
- room service with no logic,
- and the button… on overdrive.

At reception, the counter had four computers.

On a night like that, none of them were ever idle.

Nikos and Michele up front—switching between PMS, charges, phone calls.

Alejandro moving between the lobby and the elevators. Ramon had already gone upstairs—room service delays. Papa-Nikos held the kitchen and the back corridor, because someone had to.

I was in the back office. Two computers. One for reports. One for damages, incidents, numbers. Someone always stays behind.

Always.

02:47 a.m.

Ding.

The red light came on.

Michele picked up the handset with both hands.

"Reception, good evening."

Silence.

Nikos looked at him.

"Don't talk," I whispered from behind. "Let them."

"Hello… can you hear me?"

"Yes, sir."

"What time does breakfast start?"

Nikos typed mechanically.

"From 7:00."

"Thank you."

Click.

Alejandro walked past.

"First call always stupid," he said. "Tradition."

He didn't even finish—

Ding.

"Sorry to bother you…"

Michele looked at me, panicked.

"This sentence… bad, yes?"

I nodded.

"The Wi-Fi isn't working."

"Would you like us to check it?"

"No, I just wanted you to know."

Click.

From the inside, Papa-Nikos' voice carried:

"Know it for what reason? So we can be sad about it?"

Ding.

"The room next door is making noise."

Ramon's voice came through the radio:

"I'm near. I check."

Someone always stays behind at reception in case something else happens.

Two minutes later—

Ding.

"Now it's worse."

Alejandro smiled, tired.

"They want witness. Not silence."

Nikos wrote down the room number.

A room service call—

And then…

Ding.

"Can you bring me a charger?"
"No."
"A cable?"
"No."
"A pillow?"
"Yes."
"A glass?"
"Yes."
"Ice?"
"We'll try."
"And a painkiller?"

Michele lifted his head.

"Here… we stop, yes?"

"Here we stop," Papa-Nikos said. "If you don't stop here, next he'll ask for a doctor."

Quiet laughter. Exhausted.

And then—

Ding.

A different sound.

"Reception!"

"Yes—tell me."

"My husband won't wake up."

No one spoke.

Ramon stayed on the floor.
Alejandro grabbed the radio.
Nikos stayed at the desk.
Michele stared at me.
Papa-Nikos took the keys.

We don't all leave.

Never.

"I'm calling an ambulance," I said.

"Let's go."

When everything was over, the button was still
there.

Small.
Plastic.
Innocent.

338 rooms.

338 stories.

And always someone behind the counter. Because at night, it doesn't matter who runs. It matters who can stand to stay.

CHAPTER 5

Love, Desire, and Room Service

If there is one chapter no hotel manual would ever dare to write, it's this one.

Because love in hotels doesn't look like love outside them. It's faster. More discreet. More honest — or much more fake. And almost always… it passes through reception.

The People Who Don't Sleep Together at Home

At night, they all come downstairs.

Not always for check-in. Mostly for excuses.

Politicians with "meetings."
Businessmen with "early mornings."
DJs with "friends."
Men who greet you like you're old buddies.

"Hey Gianni, how's the shift going?"

Like they're preparing you.

Like they're saying: *remember who I am — but don't remember what I'm doing.*

No one leaves a tip. Everyone leaves implications.

The only thing they truly ask for is discretion.

When Staff Forget They're at Work

Christmas staff party.

Everyone dancing. I'm on shift.

I walk into the men's bathroom.

A colleague comes out with another colleague.

Potso-potso.
An Italian-Spanish-Filipino word. An international word that means **sex**.

I wash my hands. I look down. A used condom. A bit of white powder. I saw nothing. I heard nothing. There are human weaknesses.

And the night forgives them — up to a point.

Because Love Always Passes Through Reception

Whatever guests think, reception is a witness.

It sees:

- who came in with whom
- who left alone
- who came down wearing sunglasses at six a.m.
- who never made eye contact

And the night manager doesn't judge.

He just remembers.

Because at night:

- love doesn't ask permission

- desire leaves no receipt
- and room service isn't always food

And me?

I was just there to open doors.

Not emotional ones.

Real ones.

Night 26 – Love, Desire, and Room Service

Saturday night. Full house.

Love in hotels never starts romantically. It usually starts with a phone call.

I was in the back office. Ramon on the floors. Alejandro in the lobby. Michele at the desk — sweating without having done anything.

02:19 a.m.

Ding.

Michele jumped.

"Reception, good evening!"

The voice on the other end was low.

Very low.

"Uh… good evening… could we order room service?"

Michele looked at me.

Confirmation mode: **ON**.

I nodded.

"Of course, sir. What would you like?"

Pause.

Small.
Uncomfortable.

"Champagne."

Alejandro raised an eyebrow.

"And… strawberries."

Ramon's voice crackled over the radio.

"Ah… romantic floor."

"Of course, sir."

"And… two glasses."

Michele typed carefully, like he was performing surgery.

"And… sorry… do you have candles?"

Silence.

Michele looked at me, panicked.

"Candle… we have candle?"

Alejandro smiled devilishly.

"We have light. Love make candle."

"Unfortunately, no candles, sir," Michele said.

"No problem," the voice replied. "We improvise."

Click.

Michele slowly put the phone down.

"This… is normal, yes?"

"Welcome to central London," I said.

Ramon came down to pick up the tray.

"Knock once," he said. "If they don't answer, I never knock again."

Two minutes later—

Ding.

Same voice.

Less quiet. Much more enthusiastic.

"Sorry… could you bring… another bottle?"

Alejandro laughed.

"Round two."

"Of course, sir."

Michele typed, hands shaking.

"Boss… charge is correct, yes?"

"Yes, Michele. Love is non-refundable."

Ramon went up again.

"This time," he said, "door open fast."

He barely made it back down.

Ding.

Different room.

"Reception, the room next door is making noise."

Alejandro closed his eyes.

"Love is loud."

"What kind of noise, sir?"

"…Passion."

Michele looked at the ceiling.

"Is… passion a complaint category?"

"Yes," I said. "And it never wins."

Ramon spoke calmly over the radio.

"I talk polite."

He went up.

Knocked.

A man opened with a grin from ear to ear.

“Sorry, sorry.”

“No problem,” Ramon said. “Just… lower happiness a bit.”

He came back down.

Two minutes of silence.

Michele smiled for the first time.

“We survive?”

Ding.

“Reception… uh… can you also bring chocolate?”

Alejandro exploded.

“This is not a hotel. This is honeymoon package!”

I messaged Ramon: *last trip.*

When it was finally over, the lobby calmed down.

Michele sat back.

“Night shift… very intense.”

Alejandro winked.

“Day shift people fall in love. Night shift people deliver it.”

I looked at the button. Quiet. For now. Because in hotels, love never sleeps.

It just orders after midnight.

Night 27 – The Lobby That Never Keeps Secrets

The lobby was quiet.

Always suspicious.

Papa-Nikos was at the bar, doing what he considered an essential part of the night shift: cleaning.

Not rushed.

Not sloppy.

First the counter. Then the stools. Then the vacuum between chairs and tables, with the precision of someone who had done this a thousand times.

Not barista work.

Night receptionist work.

What doesn't get cleaned during the day, gets cleaned at night. What others don't have time for, gets handled by the shift no one sees.

"Ready for the morning," he muttered.

Not for guests. For the next shift.

A few meters away, Nikos stood behind reception, glued to the PMS screen.

Doing night bills like he was defusing a bomb.

Every click careful. Every charge double-checked. Some triple-checked.

"Papa-Nikos," he said without looking up, "does room 214 have minibar included?"

Papa-Nikos didn't stop vacuuming.

"If they drank it," he said calmly,

"then it is."

"That's not an option in the PMS," Nikos replied.

From the back office, coffee in hand, I watched them through the glass like a late-night series.

Nikos clicked again.

"Okay… I charged it."

Pause.

"…I think."

Papa-Nikos turned off the vacuum slowly.

"Do you think… or do you know?"

"Well, the system accepted it."

"The system accepts many things," he said.

"Doesn't mean it agrees."

Nikos stared at the screen.

"What if it's wrong?"

Papa-Nikos shrugged.

"Someone will shout in the morning. Then the sun will rise. And then… we continue."

A guest walked through the lobby in pyjamas and socks. Looked at both of them, nodded like this was perfectly normal, and disappeared toward the elevators.

Nikos whispered:

"Did you see that?"

Papa-Nikos nodded.

"Local lobby wildlife."

Nikos sighed.

"Night shift is stressful."

Papa-Nikos smiled.

"No. Night is honest. Day pretends. Night survives."

Suddenly, the printer started printing by itself.

Nikos jumped.

"What did I do again?!"

Papa-Nikos didn't blink.

"Nothing. It smells fear."

The printer stopped.

Silence.

They looked at each other.

Then laughed.

Quietly. Tired. That laugh that only exists after three.

A few minutes later, Nikos closed the PMS.

"Done," he said proudly.

Papa-Nikos nodded.

"Good. You're officially a child of the night."

They grabbed their jackets.

"Smoke?" Nikos asked.

Papa-Nikos pulled out the lighter.

"Smoke."

From the back office, I watched them leave through the back door, more relaxed, smoke waiting for them, the lobby left alone again.

Bar clean. Bills done. Another night survived. And in the morning, no one would know how much work it took for absolutely nothing to happen.

Night 28 – Two Ways to Love the Night

The night had that temperature that confuses everything. Not cold. Not warm.

Something in between — like a look held a little too long.

Alejandro stood in the lobby, jacket loose, smile always ready. Spanish. Passionate. A man who loves women — and shows it.

As for men… no one was sure. Not even him.

Michele stood behind the desk.

Clean. Polished.

Not loud. Not performative.

Just… real.

Both professionals to the bone.

I was in the back office, watching them.

Not supervising. Appreciating.

02:33 a.m.

Ding.

Room service.

Michele answered.

"Reception, good evening."

The voice was low. Warm.

Two people. One room.

"We'd like… champagne."

Alejandro raised an eyebrow and smiled.

"And something… sweet."

Michele nodded to himself.

"Of course."

He hung up.

"Love call," Alejandro said.

"My favorite."

Michele smiled.

"Different kind of love," he said.

"But still love."

Alejandro looked at him a second too long.

"You always so calm," he said.

"How you do it?"

Michele shrugged.

"I don't chase. I recognize."

Alejandro laughed.

"In Spain, we chase. Hard."

"I can see that," Michele said. "Every night."

A couple passed through the lobby, hand in hand, laughing softly.

Alejandro watched them like someone who believes in love as an event, not an idea.

"I like nights like this," he said.

"People remember they are alive."

Michele closed the PMS.

"I like nights when people are kind," he said.

"Even when they're loud."

Silence.

Not awkward.

Beautiful.

Alejandro leaned on the counter.

"You happy, Michele?"

Michele looked at him clearly.

"Yes. Exactly where I want to be."

Alejandro nodded slowly.

"Good answer."

Room service went up. Champagne popped somewhere above. Laughter drifted down the corridors.

The night continued.

Later, I watched them work side by side.

No tension. No competition.

Two different ways of loving.

Same respect.

At **04:01 a.m.**, Alejandro broke the silence.

"You know… love isn't the same for everyone."

Michele smiled.

"But work is."

They were both right.

Because in hotel nights, love changes shape, desire changes voice, but respect… respect always stays the same.

Night 29 – Training, Hunger, and Salmon at 03:00

This night was supposed to be quiet.

That was the first mistake.

It was a training shift.

Papa-Nikos was beside me, learning how the night really works.

Not how manuals describe it.

How it happens.

Ramon and Alejandro were on shift with us.

Which meant two things:

1. The hotel would survive.
2. Someone would get hungry.

At **01:20 a.m.**, Papa-Nikos began to suffer.

Not discreetly.

"I'm fine," he said, standing suspiciously close to the drawers.

"I'm not hungry."

Alejandro smiled instantly.

"In Spain," he said, "when a man says 'I'm not hungry,' he is already late."

Papa-Nikos opened one drawer. Closed it. Opened another.

"I ate earlier," he said.

Ramon looked at him calmly.

"Yes," he replied. "Yesterday."

I watched without speaking.

That was part of the training.

"Lesson one," I said.

"Never lie about hunger on night shift."

At **02:00 a.m.**, Ramon disappeared toward the kitchen.

No announcement.

No questions.

Purpose.

"Lesson two," I said.

"When Ramon goes to the kitchen, you don't ask why."

Alejandro nodded seriously.

"He goes to solve problems," he said.

"Sometimes food. Sometimes people."

Ten minutes later, Ramon returned.

Not with snacks.

With a plate.

A real plate.

Salmon.
Potatoes.
Vegetables.
Steaming.

He placed it in front of Papa-Nikos.

"For everyone," he said.

"But you first."

Papa-Nikos stared like it was a miracle.

"We're training," he said weakly.

"You're hungry," Ramon replied.

Training paused.

Papa-Nikos sat down.

Ate.

Silence.

The good kind.

"Lesson three," I said.

"Night shift is teamwork. Not heroics."

Of course, the hotel couldn't tolerate peace.

02:47 a.m.

The phone rang.

A guest complained the air conditioning was "too cold and too hot."

Alejandro took the call.

"So… temperature-confused?" he asked politely.

The guest didn't laugh.

Alejandro went upstairs.

Ramon stayed behind.

Someone had to guard the salmon.

Five minutes later, Alejandro returned.

"What was it?" Papa-Nikos asked between bites.

"AC on. Window open," Alejandro said.

"The hotel was arguing with itself."

"Who won?" Papa-Nikos asked.

"The hotel," Alejandro said. "Always."

At **03:30 a.m.**, the lobby settled.

Papa-Nikos leaned back, full and calmer.

"So… this job isn't just reception," he said.

I smiled.

"No," I replied.

"It's management, psychology, emergencies… and sometimes catering."

Ramon washed the plate.
Alejandro checked the lobby.
Papa-Nikos nodded slowly.

"I get it," he said.

"Then," I replied,

"training is going well."

Some nights teach you procedures. Others make you more human. This night taught both.

Night 30 – The Tip

The Russian and the 200 Euros

During the day, he was a gentleman. At night… he was someone else.

He had arrived with his wife. Breakfast together. Smiles. Politeness.

A man in his mid-thirties. Well dressed. Calm. The kind who doesn't draw attention.

But at night, inside a hotel, people change.

He came down to the reception a little after midnight. Alone.

He approached without hurry. Rested his hand on the desk. Then pulled 200 euros from his pocket.

He placed them in front of me. Like a tip.

"I go outside," he said.

"You watch my wife."

It wasn't a question. It was an order.

I froze for a second. Not out of fear. Out of surprise.

"Excuse me?" I said.

He looked at me calmly. Smiling.

"I want to be alone. You make sure nobody goes to the room."

The 200 euros stayed there.

Still.

"Okay, sir," I replied.

"Tomorrow," he said.

"Tomorrow we speak again."

And he left.

The next night, he came down again.

Same time.

Same smile.

He left another 200 euros on the desk.

"I work for the Russian mafia," he said quietly. "I sell drugs in Saint Petersburg."

I didn't change my expression. You learn early that at night, if you react, you lose.

"I have rooms in all hotels around," he continued. "Nobody knows where I stay."

I didn't answer.

I just looked at him.

"You understand?"

I understood something very simple: this man wanted to feel powerful. And a hotel at night is the perfect stage for that.

"Sir," I said calmly,

"I work here so people can sleep peacefully. That's all."

He looked at me for a few seconds. As if weighing whether it was worth continuing.

"Good night," he finally said.

And went upstairs.

Roxie in the Taxi

I thought the story was over.

In my mind, the Russian had left my life the way most night guests do: without explanation, without a sequel.

I was wrong.

It was a little after three when the entrance door opened again. Not from the inside. From outside.

His voice entered the lobby before he did.

"Mr. Giannis! My friend! Come out!"

He wasn't shouting. He was calling. As if we knew each other. I raised my head slowly. I didn't rush. At night, if you rush, it means the rope is pulling you.

"I found a good one!" he said, laughing.

I stepped toward the door.

The taxi was parked right outside. And in the back seat, legs crossed, eyes tired, was Roxie.

Black.

From Nigeria.

She worked in a strip club.

We knew her. Not by name, but by presence.

She was one of those "visitors" who don't need introductions.

The hotel had seen many like her. But every time, the atmosphere changed. She looked at me. Recognized me. Smiled lightly, without a trace of shame.

"Hi baby," she said.

It wasn't an invitation. It was formality.

I looked at the Russian. He was happy. Childishly happy. Like someone who thinks he's won something.

"Good night, sir," I said.

"Enjoy your night."

He didn't mention money again. He didn't mention his wife again.

In the morning, he came down with his wife. A gentleman. Polite. As if nothing had happened.

That's when I understood something no manual teaches you:

At night, in a hotel, you don't guard rooms. You guard roles. Everyone plays their own. And you have to stay in yours. Even when 200 euros land on the desk. Even if that week, I made two months' salary.

Night 31 – Seafood

The Lobster and the Octopus

It was one of those nights when the lobby laughs by itself. No reason. No music.

Two Swedish girls had come down earlier.
Tall.
Blonde.
With that smile you can't tell is innocent or dangerous. Every time the groom walked by, they laughed.

Not loudly.

In sync.

The groom was one of those who stand out.
Tall.

Fit.
Amateur football player.

And—most importantly— he had no idea what was coming.

A little after three, the phone rang.

"Room service," they said.

"We want to order."

"Of course. What would you like?" I replied.

A short pause.

Then laughter.

"The groom is the lobster." "And you are the octopus."

I looked at the receiver. There was no guideline for that in the manual.

"Excuse me?" I said.

"We want the lobster upstairs.

For one hour."

"One hour?" I asked out of habit.

"Immediately," they said, and hung up.

I stood still for a few seconds. Then I called the groom.

"Go upstairs."

“What?”
“No man… I’m in a relationship.”
“I don’t care,” I said.
“They asked for you.”

He looked at me like he was trying to figure out if I was joking.

“Man… seriously?”

“Very seriously.”

And he went.

The Swedes and the Groom

He came back half an hour later.
Quiet.
Pale.
Like someone who had returned from another dimension.

“What happened?” I asked.

He sat on the couch.

“I walk in… One is naked. Wrapped in a towel. The other is on the bed.”

He stopped.

Swallowed.

“They tell me ‘sit.’

I sit. Then the friend pulls off the towel. She starts touching me. Blowjob. Both of them.”

He looked up.

"I finished."

I looked at him.

"What do you mean, 'finished'?"

"I didn't fuck them," he said.

"Only blowjob."

There was silence.

"And then?" I asked.

"They say 'thank you.'

They kiss me.

And I leave."

I looked at him the way you look at someone who doesn't know what just happened to him.

"Man…" I finally said.

"That's luck."

He didn't laugh.

"It wasn't how you imagine," he said.

"It was… strange."

He stood up.

Went back to his post.

The Swedish girls never appeared in the lobby again. In the morning, they left smiling. Calm. As if nothing had happened.

That's when I understood something true in every hotel at night:

Love doesn't ask permission. Passion leaves no receipt. And the staff, if they're not careful, can very easily forget that they are working.

Night 32 – The Invitation with the Towels

The night had that relaxed smell Saturdays get after two. No tension. No problems. Just promises.

I was doing the floor check mechanically. Keys in hand. Radio turned down. My mind half at work, half at dawn.

At the corner of the corridor, I heard laughter. Not loud. Not disturbing. The kind that carries alcohol and confidence.

The door opened before I could knock.

Two women. Towels loosely wrapped around them. Wet hair. Steam coming from the bathroom.

"Come in," one of them said.

Not an invitation.

A statement.

I stood there. The corridor empty behind me. The door half open. The night waiting to see what I'd do.

"Routine floor check," I said.

My voice normal.
Not strict.
Not relaxed.
The other one laughed.

"Come on… five minutes."

I didn't move closer. I didn't step away. Some moments aren't for quick decisions. They're for not making mistakes.

"I can't," I said.

"If you need anything, call reception."

They looked at me for a second longer than necessary. Not disappointed. More… curious.

"Okay," one of them said.

"Too bad."

They closed the door. The corridor returned to its silence. I continued the check. I didn't feel like a hero. I didn't feel like a loser.

Just something simple and clear:

There are nights when the hardest "no" isn't said out of fear or rules. It's said so you can stand behind the desk in the morning and not have to lower your eyes.

Night 33 – The Staff Who Forgot They Were Working

The problem with night staff isn't fatigue. It's that sometimes they forget why they're there.

It was a little after three. That hour when everything seems under control—and that's exactly why people relax. The groom wasn't at his post.

Not the first time.

Usually he takes a round, a cigarette outside, comes back. This time, he was late. I heard voices from the back of the lobby. Not arguing. Laughter.

I walked toward the bar. It was closed, but the fridge light always stayed on. I saw him there. With two female guests.

Sitting on the stools. Drinks in hand. Not hiding. Not rushed.

As if there were no hotel around them.

I stood there for a second without speaking. They hadn't seen me.

"So then?" one of them said, laughing.

The groom laughed too. Leaning forward, elbow on the bar.

Then he saw me.

His smile stopped abruptly. Not from fear. From realization.

"Uh… everything okay?" he said.

"Yes," I replied.

"You're working."

I didn't shout.

I didn't change my tone.

That confused him more than anything.

The girls looked at me.

A moment of awkwardness.

Then they stood up.

"Good night," they said.

And headed for the elevator.

The groom stayed standing.

"I didn't do anything wrong," he said.

"We were just talking."

"I know," I replied.

"But you weren't talking like you were working."

He lowered his eyes.

Not much.

Just enough to show he heard me.

"If you want to flirt," I continued,

"pick a time when you're not wearing a uniform."

He didn't answer.

"Go back to your post."

He left without a word.

I stayed alone in the lobby. The fridge closed. The light went out. I thought about how easily the line blurs. Not between right and wrong. But between

"I'm a human" and "I have responsibility."

Because at night, it's not enough to be present. You have to remember who you are and why. And sometimes, that's harder than anything else.

Night 34 – The Condom in the Lobby Bathroom

The lobby bathrooms are one of those places nobody notices. Until there's a reason.

It was just before four when the woman came to reception. Not angry. Not shocked. Just... uncomfortable.

"Excuse me," she said quietly. "There's something in the bathroom."

"What exactly?" I asked.

She hesitated.

"Uh… a condom."

She didn't say "used."

She didn't have to.

"Thank you for telling us," I said.

"We'll take care of it."

She nodded, relieved. She didn't want to discuss it. She just wanted to leave that moment behind. I took gloves. Paper. Went there.

The condom was there. Next to the sink. Not carelessly thrown away. As if someone had left it on purpose.

I stood there for a moment before calling Ramon to clean it. Not out of disgust. Out of thought.

Lobby bathrooms aren't rooms. They're not private space. They're passageways.

Someone came down. Someone didn't wait. Someone thought no one would see.

Ramon came—Filipino, good guy, solid colleague. We cleaned. Disinfected. Everything as it should be.

Back behind the desk, I thought about how many things people leave behind at night. Not objects. Decisions. And how often the night shift isn't asked to judge. Just to clean up.

In the morning, the bathrooms would be spotless again. No one would know. No one would ask.

But I would remember.

Because at night, not everything is a scandal. Some things are just traces. And someone has to be there to erase them without asking how or why they were made.

Night 35 – The Room That Didn't Leave a Tip

A tip isn't an obligation. But when it's missing, you feel it. Not in the money. In the way.

It was a little after six. The night was starting to deflate. The lobby smelled like coffee from the waking kitchen.

The groom came back from the floor. He didn't say anything. Just parked the trolley and stood there for a moment.

"Room 612," he finally said.

He didn't need to say more.

"Nothing?" I asked.

He shook his head.

"Not a euro."

He took a breath.

"And it's not just that…"

He looked up.

"Twice upstairs. Drinks, ice, towels. Smiles. Thank you. Everything."

I didn't comment.

"How was the room?" I asked.

He smiled crookedly.

"Like a storm passed through. Sheets on the floor. Towels everywhere. And the minibar… empty."

"Charged?"

"Everything."

That was all that mattered.

The groom went to the lockers. He wasn't angry. It was something else. Like he felt someone owed him acknowledgment.

I stayed alone.

I thought about how strange tipping is. It doesn't buy service. It buys emotion.

And some people never pay for that part. Not because they can't. But because they don't understand it.

In the morning, the room would be cleaned. Accounts closed. Everything technically correct. But something small would remain. Not in the system. In people. Because at night, you don't only count what guests took. You also count what they left behind.

Night 36 – The Morning Look of Shame

Morning forgives nothing. Whatever happened at night, it brings into the light without filters. It was just before seven. The morning shift was gathering behind the desk. Coffee. Low voices. That fake freshness.

I was still there. I hadn't left.

He came down first. Slow. Hands in his pockets. Sunglasses, though there was no sun yet. He didn't look around. Didn't look at me. Went straight to the bar for water.

Drank it standing. Like medicine.

A few minutes later, she came down.

Hair loosely tied. No makeup. Eyes lowered.

She stood for a moment. As if considering going back. She didn't.

She approached the desk.

"Good morning," she said.

"Good morning," I replied.

Her voice was normal. That's what gave her away.

She handed over the key. Didn't ask anything. Didn't request anything. The man stood farther away. Waiting.

They didn't exchange a word. Didn't exchange a glance. The receipt printed. She took it without looking.

"Thank you," she said.

"Have a good day," I replied.

For a fraction of a second, she lifted her head. Our eyes met.

It wasn't shame for what happened. It was shame that it was over. She turned. Left.

The man followed a few steps behind. Not together. Never together.

The door closed.

The morning shift continued as if nothing had happened. And indeed, for the hotel, nothing had happened.

But I knew this:

Night leaves marks that don't show on rooms. They show only in looks. And in the morning, when everything looks clean, those are what reveal what really passed through here.

Night 37 – The Woman Who Left Alone

Not everyone left together that morning. Some people always leave alone, even if they didn't arrive that way.

It was a little after seven. Sunlight was entering the lobby through the big windows. The kind of light that forgives nothing.

She came down with a small suitcase. Not hers. You could tell by the way she held it.

She looked around. Not searching for someone. More like confirming he wasn't there.

She approached the desk.

"Check-out," she said.

She didn't smile. She didn't seem angry. She was calm in a final way.

"Name?" I asked.

She gave it to me. The room was under someone else's name.

"One moment," I said.

Behind me, the morning shift pretended not to hear. Everyone knows when not to look.

I checked the account. Everything paid.

"Receipt?"

She shook her head.

"No.
I don't need it."

I kept the card in the drawer a second longer than necessary. No reason. Maybe to give her time.

"Would you like a taxi?"

She looked up.

"No.
I'll walk a bit."

I placed the key in its holder.

Closed the folio.

"Take care," I said.

She looked at me properly for the first time.

"Thank you," she said.

"For everything."

I didn't ask what she meant.

She turned. Went through the door.The suitcase made that small sound on the pavement.

I watched her walk away. Without looking back.

Some stories don't have farewell scenes. They only have exits. And at night, that's enough to know something ended without ever being said.

Night 38 – The Love That Was Never Written

They never spoke. Not at check-in. Not in the elevator. Not when they took the key from my hand. They stood in front of the desk like people waiting in line for something they weren't sure they wanted.

"Good evening," I said.

They both nodded. Not together. Not with the same rhythm.

The name was in the system. One room. One night. I handed over the card. He took it. She didn't reach out.

"The elevator is to the right," I said.

They didn't say thank you. Not out of rudeness. Out of concentration. Like they were afraid that if they spoke, something would break.

I saw them again later. Just before three.

They came down for water. Stood side by side. Touching, but not touching.

She looked at the floor.

He looked at his watch.

"Everything okay?" I asked, out of habit.

"Yes," he said.

She didn't speak.

They went back to the room without looking back. At night, "just one night" is never said out loud. It's signed silently. It doesn't need promises. It doesn't need a future.

It only needs no one to ask, "and then what?"

In the morning, they came down separately.

She first. Early. Coat closed all the way up, though it wasn't cold.

"Check-out," she said.

Her name wasn't on the room.

I didn't comment.

"Receipt?"
"No."

She stayed a second longer.

"The key…"

"You left it inside," I said.

She nodded.

"Thank you."

It was the first word she spoke.

She left.

He came down later.

Unhurried.
No expression.

"She left?" he asked.

He didn't say a name. He didn't need to.

"Yes," I replied.

He took the card from his pocket.

Placed it on the counter.

"Okay."

That was all.

When the lobby emptied, I thought something simple: Some nights don't leave stains on the sheets. They leave only silence. And that silence isn't written in an incident report. It isn't charged. It isn't explained.

It just… passes.

Like loves that were never spoken. And that's why they never needed to end.

CHAPTER 6

Security Issues (According to the Guest)

If you ask a guest what a "security issue" is, they'll tell you about noise, about someone looking suspicious, about an argument they might have heard. If you ask a night manager, they'll tell you something else.

A security issue is what you can't take back. What can't be fixed with an apology. What doesn't fit easily into an incident report.

When Security Is Not About Rules

There are other "security issues."

Police in the lobby. Three guests with backpacks. Hands on the wall. Search.

Weed. A lot of it.

In London, the smell means nothing. Quantity means everything.

The groom goes up to their room. Comes back down with another small bag.

"Boss?"
"Throw it away. We don't get involved."

He smiled. The shiny tooth showed. Did he keep it? I don't know. In the morning, the police came again. They searched. They found things. They left.

Everything was written in the incident report. As it should be.

What "Security" Really Means

The guest thinks security is:

- cameras
- guards
- locked doors

The night manager knows security is:

- decisions made in seconds
- human judgment
- staying calm when everything around freezes

And sometimes… it's accepting that you did what you could. And that has to be enough.

Night 39 – "Security as It Really Is"

Most people think security is about muscles. Wrong. At night, security is about timing.

It was a little after three when he came into the lobby. He wasn't running. He wasn't looking around.

That's what worried me.

He stood near the entrance. Not at the desk. As if he didn't want it to look like he was asking for something.

"Good evening," I said.

He turned slowly.

"Good evening," he replied.

"I'm waiting."

"For someone?"

"Yes."

I didn't ask who. When someone wants to tell you, they do. Five minutes passed. Ten.

He didn't leave.

There was no arrival in the system. No reservation. No note.

"Can I help you with something?" I asked again.

He looked at me properly for the first time.

"I have an appointment," he said.

"In a room."

"Which room?"

He stopped.

"They didn't give me a number."

That was it.

"Without a name or room number, I can't let you wait here," I said.

"If you want, you can call the person you're meeting."

He smiled slightly.

"He'll be a little late."

"Then you'll have to wait outside."

The smile faded.

"I'm not making noise," he said.

"I'm not bothering anyone."

"I know," I replied.

"But that doesn't mean you can stay."

He looked at me for a few seconds. Not angry. Calculating.

"You decide?" he asked.

"Yes."

That was all.

I didn't raise my voice. I didn't step back.

He finally turned toward the door. Paused for a second.

"Have a good shift," he said.

"Take care," I replied.

He left.

The door closed. The lobby stayed quiet. Nothing happened. And that was exactly the point. Because security at night isn't reacting to what happened. It's understanding in time what must not happen.

And stopping it without shouting, without a scene, without anyone applauding.

Night 40 – The Groom and the Small Bag

The problem wasn't the bag. It was the look.

It was past four when I saw him enter the lobby through the side door. Not the main one. The staff entrance.

He was walking a little faster than usual. Not anxious. Focused.

"Everything okay?" I asked.

He stopped abruptly. As if he hadn't expected the question.

"Yes," he said.

Too fast.

His hand was closed. Not clenched. Protective.

"Come here," I said.

He didn't react. But his hand dropped lower. He stopped in front of the desk.

"What do you have?" I asked.

"Nothing."

He didn't smile. He didn't joke.

That was his mistake.

"Open your hand," I said.

He looked around.

The lobby was empty.

He opened his palm.

A small bag. Transparent. Not enough to sell. Enough to get you in trouble.

"Where did it come from?" I asked.

"A guest," he said.

"He asked me to throw it away."

Yes, these little "gifts" happen in London.

"You know this can't happen," I said.

He nodded.

"I didn't keep it," he said.

"I brought it to you."

That's what saved him.

I put on gloves. Took an evidence bag. By the book.

"It won't be written up," I told him.

"Not to burn you.

To protect you."

He understood.

"Sorry," he said.

"It's not about being sorry," I replied.

"It's about personal boundaries."

The bag left the desk. The night went on. The groom returned to his post. A little quieter. A little smaller.

And I thought about something you won't find in an SOP:

Security isn't tested only by guests. It's tested by the people working next to you. And if you don't hold the line there, it doesn't matter how many doors you locked correctly.

Because the night always enters from the inside.

Night 41 – The Guest in the Corridor

At night, anything that doesn't belong in a room stands out immediately.

It was just before four when the phone rang. Not from a room. From a floor.

"There's someone outside our door," the voice said. "He's just standing there."

They didn't say "shouting."

They didn't say "knocking."

That was worse.

"Which room?" I asked.

They told me.

I took the radio. Called the groom.

We went upstairs.

The corridor was dimly lit.

Silent.

And then we saw him.

Sitting on the floor. Back against the wall. Knees pulled in. He wasn't sleeping. He wasn't crying. He was staring at the door across from him.

"Good evening," I said.

He didn't turn.

"Sir?"

He slowly lifted his head.

"I don't want to go in," he said.

"But I can't leave."

I didn't answer right away.

"Which room is yours?" I asked.

He pointed.

"There."

"Do you need help?"

He shook his head.

"I just want to sit for a bit."

I looked at the groom. He looked back at me.

"You can't stay here," I said.

"But we can go downstairs."

He didn't react. Didn't argue. He stood up slowly. As if it cost him something. In the elevator, he didn't speak. In the lobby, he sat in a chair.

I gave him water.

"Everything okay?" I asked.

He looked at the glass.

"No."

"Do you want us to call someone?"

"No."

"Do you want to change rooms?"

He looked up properly for the first time.

"No," he said.

"I just want it to pass."

I didn't ask what.

He stayed a while.

Then stood up on his own.

"Thank you," he said.

"Sorry for the trouble."

He went upstairs.

The corridor emptied.

The door closed.

There was no incident. No report.

But I knew: Sometimes security isn't about removing someone. It's about moving them to a place where they don't scare anyone. And letting them pull themselves together without an audience.

Night 42 – The Wallet in His Hand

He wasn't holding the wallet like an object. He was holding it like a decision.

It was a little after five when I saw him approach the desk slowly. He wasn't in a hurry. He wasn't looking around. He stopped in front of me and placed the wallet on the counter. Not to pay. To show it.

"I found it," he said.

"Where?" I asked.

“In the elevator.”

He opened it himself.

Didn’t look inside.

Just enough to show the ID.

“It’s not mine.”

“I know,” I said.

“Thank you.”

He didn’t let go.

“How much do you get if I turn it in here?” he asked.

Not sarcastic.

Practical.

“Nothing,” I replied.

He smiled slightly.

“Then why not keep it?”

I didn’t change my tone.

“You can keep it,” I said.

“But then tomorrow morning you won’t be able to look at yourself in the mirror without thinking about it.”

He went silent.

Closed the wallet. Pushed it toward me.

"Not everyone is like that," he said.

"I know," I replied.

"That's why the ones who are stand out."

He stayed a second longer.

As if waiting for something.

"You'll find him?" he asked.

"Yes."

"Good."

He turned and left.

I opened the wallet alone.

Name.
Room.
Cards.

I knocked.

"Reception."

The door opened almost immediately.

"You lost this," I said.

His eyes filled before he could speak.

"Yes."

I handed it over.

"Someone found it in the elevator."

"Thank you," he said.

"Thank you so much."

He closed the door slowly.

Back at the desk, I thought about how thin the line is. Not between right and wrong. Between easy and honest. And how often at night people place that line in your hand and wait to see what you'll do.

Night 43 – The Incident Report That Couldn't Hold It All

Some incidents are easy to write. Others don't fit on the form.

It was a little after five when I sat down to write. The night had calmed on the surface. But inside, it carried a lot.

I opened the system.

Time.
Floor.
Room.

I started.

"During the night shift…"

I stopped.

Which night?

The one with the backpacks? The one with the groom? The one with the man in the corridor? The one with the wallet?

All of them were correct. All of them isolated. And all of them together were the problem.

I kept writing.

Facts.
Not thoughts.

Not conclusions.

I deleted.

Rewrote.

The "Comments" field filled quickly.

Too quickly.

I had to choose what stayed. And what disappeared.

You can't write: "The man wasn't dangerous, just lost."

You can't write: "The groom was more afraid than he admitted."

You can't write: "If I had taken one step differently, everything would be different."

I wrote only what the paper could handle.

Time.
Actions.
Outcome.

I saved.

The report closed. The night didn't. I stood up. Looked at the lobby.

Everything looked calm. Clean. Under control.

But I knew:

Incident reports aren't written to remember what happened. They're written so no one ever sees how much didn't happen. And the night manager learns to live with what stayed outside the form. Because that's where all the responsibility fits.

The Fear That Doesn't Show

Real fear on the night shift doesn't shout. Doesn't run. Doesn't call for help.

It stands quietly inside you, while everyone around believes that "nothing happened." It's the fear of the mistake that won't show immediately. Of the decision you made alone. Of the person you sent away or kept without knowing what they would have done if you had given them five more minutes.

No one sees it. But it decides everything.

The Night That Froze

There are nights that don't unfold.

They just… freeze.

Not because something big happened. But because everything was about to. That's when you understand that the hardest part of security isn't action.

It's waiting. Standing still. Not rushing. Not panicking. Not relaxing.

Responsibility Without Applause

No one will congratulate you for what you prevented.

There's no report for the incident that didn't happen. No email for the fight that never started. No reward for the door that stayed closed.

Responsibility at night is silent. And if you do it right, it looks like you were never there.

Security as It Really Is

Security isn't cameras. It isn't muscles. It isn't shouting. It's decisions made in low light.It's reading looks before they speak. It's the calm "no" that doesn't invite argument.

And above all, it's being able in the morning to hand over the shift without having to explain why everything went "normally." Because when everything looks normal, it means you did your job.

CHAPTER 7

Alcohol, Bad Decisions, and the Night Shift

If there's one sentence I've heard more than any other at night, it's this: "I'm not that drunk."

It's always said by the drunkest ones.

Alcohol doesn't change people. It just strips them.

And on the night shift, you see things that during the day hide behind ties, smiles, and polite "good mornings."

The Heroes of the Return

Around two, they start coming back.

Some from bars.
Some from clubs.
Some from places they'll never name.

They enter the lobby with that walk that tries to look steady. But isn't.

"Hey, my friend!"

We're not friends. But at night, everyone is looking for one.

"Everything okay?" you ask.

"Perfect. Just… "

(stumbles)
"…lost my key."

Classic.

Alcohol and Truth

I've seen people cry because their drink ran out. Others get angry because you didn't let them have another.

"Come on, man. One last one."

"Last" is always the second-to-last.

And then:

- broken glasses
- broken doors
- broken promises

A guest broke a corridor lamp. Not out of anger. Out of… balance.

"I fell by myself."

I believe him.

Bad Decisions with Good Intentions

Alcohol also brings generosity.

"Have a drink with me."

"Thanks, I can't."

"Come on, relax."

You don't relax on the night shift. You survive.

Some want to hug. Some want to explain their life. Some want to tell you why their wife doesn't understand them.

And you listen.

Because if you don't, you'll find them shouting in the corridor.

"Who Broke This?"

Alcohol has no memory.

In the morning, everyone says:

"I don't know how it happened."

And yet, it did.

Chairs moved.
Plants overturned.
A table missing a leg.

The incident report fills up.

And there's always one who remembers a little: "I think we were laughing."

Yes. That part is certain.

Fights That Start from Nothing

Two men. A look. A word. And suddenly, tension.

"What are you looking at?"

Classic opening.

That's where you step in—before it becomes something else. Not like a cop. Like someone who doesn't want to write another report.

Sometimes it works. Sometimes it doesn't.

When Alcohol Meets Responsibility

And then there are moments when the laughter stops. A drunk guest. But not funny.

You worry.

"Sir, are you okay?"

"Yeah… just…"

And he falls.

That's where alcohol stops being a story. And becomes an incident. You call for help. You keep people away.

And you think how thin the line is.

Why Alcohol Loves the Night

Alcohol finds space at night because no one judges it immediately. And a hotel is neutral ground.

You're not at home.

You're not at work.

You're somewhere in between.

And there, bad decisions feel less bad.

Until morning.

Morning Remembers. Night Doesn't.

In the morning, the same people:

- apologize
- don't remember
- leave in a hurry

And you stay behind.

With one more chapter in your memory. And one more report in the system. Because alcohol passes. Decisions stay.

And on the night shift, you're there to pick up the pieces. Not just broken objects. But people.

Night 44 – "I'm Not That Drunk"

He said it before he even reached the desk. Like a warning. Or a defense.

It was a little after two. The hour when alcohol stops being fun and starts becoming an excuse. He walked crooked. Not enough to fall. He spoke clearly. Just louder than necessary.

"I'm not that drunk," he said again.

"I just had a bit too much."

I didn't ask if he was drunk. You never need to.

"How can I help?" I asked.

He leaned his elbow on the counter. All his weight forward.

"I can't find my room."

Classic.

"Name?"

"I know… wait…"

He closed his eyes for a second. Not to remember. To stay upright.

He gave me the name. It existed. The room existed.

"Shall I walk you up?" I asked.

"No, no… I can."

That's always the wrong moment.

"I'll come with you," I said.

Not a question.

In the corridor, he walked one step ahead. Like he had something to prove. On the third step, he stumbled. Didn't fall. But he understood. He stopped. Took a breath.

"Okay… yeah."

I opened the door. He went in without speaking.

"Water?"
"Yes."

I handed him the bottle. He held it with both hands.

"Thank you," he said.

"I'm not—"

He didn't finish.

"Get some rest," I said.

I closed the door behind me.

Walking back, I thought how often "I'm not that drunk" isn't said to convince you. It's said to convince the person saying it that they still have control.

And at night, control is always lost one drink before you realize it.

Night 45 – The Broken Lamp

The sound came before the call. A crack that didn't belong in a hotel.

Then the phone.

"Reception… something fell in the room next to us."

They didn't say "broke."

They didn't say "noise."

They said fell.

"Which room?" I asked.

They told me.

I took the groom. We went up.

The corridor smelled of alcohol. Not strong. Enough.

I knocked.

"Reception."

No answer.

I knocked again.

"Reception. Is everything okay?"

Movement inside.

Footsteps.
A chair dragged.

The door opened a crack.

"Yes," a voice said.

"Everything's fine."

The lamp was visible through the gap. Broken on the floor. Exposed wire.

"Can we come in and check?" I said.

The door opened a bit more.

Two people. He standing. She sitting on the bed.

No one spoke.

"It fell by itself," he said.

"Lamps don't fall by themselves," I replied. Calmly.

He didn't react. Just looked at the floor.

"We'll need to disconnect it," I said.

"And log the damage."

"I'll pay," he said quickly.

"No problem."

There was a problem. Just not about money.

"Is everyone okay?" I asked.

The woman nodded. Not convincingly.

"Would you like to change rooms?"

"No," he said.

"It was just… a moment."

That's always the problem with alcohol. Everything is "just a moment."

We removed the lamp. Secured the wire. Logged the damage.

In the corridor, as we left, the groom looked at me.

"It wasn't an accident," he said quietly.

"I know," I replied.

"But not every mistake has to become an incident."

We went down.

I thought how easily things break at night. A lamp. A glass. A boundary. And how often, in the morning, only the broken object remains.

Not the moment that broke it.

Night 46 – A Fight Over a Look

The fight didn't start with shouting. It started with silence. It was just after two-thirty when the first man came down.

Fast.
Tight steps.

He didn't come to the desk. Went straight outside for a cigarette. Two minutes later, the second one came down. Same height. Same drink in hand. Different look.

He stood near the bar. Looked outside. Then at me.

"Did you see him?" he asked.

"Who?"
"Your friend."

I didn't answer.

"He looked at me weird earlier," he said.

"Up there."

"What do you mean?"

"Like he was looking at my wife."

These sentences don't ask for answers. They ask for allies.

"I didn't see anything," I said.

His look darkened slightly.

"He was drunk."

"Everyone is a bit," I replied.

"That doesn't mean anything."

The first man came back in. Half a cigarette. Red eyes.

They met in the middle of the lobby.

Not too close.

But not backing off.

"What were you looking at?"

"Nothing."
"Drink your drink."

I stepped forward.

"Gentlemen," I said calmly.

"There's no issue here."

No one looked at me.

"Speak when I speak to you," one said.

"I'm not talking to you," the other replied.

Alcohol doesn't need a reason. Just a spark.

"This stops here," I said.

"Now."

I raised my hand slightly. Not threatening.

Firm.

"One upstairs."

"One outside."

They looked at me.

For the first time.

One laughed ironically.

The other clenched his teeth.

"Now," I repeated.

A pause.

That pause that decides everything.

They backed off. Not because they agreed. Because they were tired. One took the elevator. The other went outside.

The lobby found its rhythm again.

I stood behind the desk.

I thought how many fights don't start from actions. But from assumptions. From a look that may never have existed. But inside a drunk mind became reason enough. And at night, sometimes, the hardest thing is stopping a fight that never had a real reason to begin.

Night 47 – The Drink That Became a Problem

It wasn't the drink. It was the second one.

It was a little after three when the bar called.

No shouting.

No tension.

"Can you come over?" the bartender said. "Something doesn't sit right."

That's always a bad sign.

People who've worked behind a bar for years don't worry easily.

I went.

The man was sitting alone.

Glass half full.

His hand still on the table.

He wasn't talking.

Wasn't looking around.

"Everything okay?" I asked.

He lifted his head slowly.

"Yeah," he said.

"I'm just… a bit dizzy."

The bartender looked at me. No explanation needed.

"How much have you had?" I asked.

"Two."

Too fast.

"Here?"
"One."

That was the problem.

We didn't know the second one.

And when you don't know what you drank before, you don't know what comes after.

"We're taking you to your room," I said.

"No need," he replied.

"I'll sit a bit."

The glass trembled slightly in his hand.

"We're going now," I said.

Not strict.

Final.

He stood up.

On the first step, his knees gave. He didn't fall.

We caught him.

"Does this happen often?" I asked.

"No," he said.

"Never."

In the elevator, he didn't speak.

Just closed his eyes.

In the room, he sat on the bed. I placed water on the nightstand.

"If it gets worse, call immediately," I said.

"Any time."

He nodded.

Leaving, I thought how sneaky alcohol is. Not when you drink a lot. When you drink carelessly. Because at night, alcohol doesn't become a problem when it ends.

It becomes a problem when you don't know where it started.

Night 48 – The Guest Who Fell

He didn't fall loudly.

It was that dull sound that isn't loud, but tightens your stomach. Just before four. The hour when legs stop obeying the mind.

I saw him exit the elevator.

Alone.
No drink in hand.

That means nothing.

Two steps. On the third, his body leaned forward.

He didn't put his hands out.

He fell.

Not badly. Not dramatically. Enough.

I ran.

"Sir?"
"Yeah… yeah… I'm fine."

They always say that.

"Stay down for a moment," I said.

I didn't try to lift him immediately. That's the second mistake.

The first is panicking.

"Any pain?"

"No… just dizzy."

The smell of alcohol was there. Not heavy. But present.

"Your head?"

"No."

"Do you remember what happened?"

"Yeah… I tripped."

He didn't. But I didn't need to say it. He stayed down a minute. Two.

"Can you stand?"

"Yes."

I helped him. Not lifting him. Supporting him.

"Do you want a doctor?"

"No."

"Should we call someone?"

"No."

The answers were the same. Clean. Almost automatic.

Ramon was already next to me.

"Let's go," I said.

We walked him up.

In the elevator, he held the rail. Not me.

In the room, he sat on the bed. I placed water beside him. Left the light on.

"If you feel dizziness, pain, confusion—call immediately."

"Okay," he said.

"Sorry."

"No need," I replied.

I closed the door.

Walking back, I thought how thin the line is between "I'm fine" and "this could have gone differently."

And how often at night, your job is to make sure someone got up. Not because they had to. But because they could.

Night 49 – Lost Balance

He didn't fall. And that was what worried me.

It was just after three-thirty when I saw him standing in the middle of the lobby.

Not walking.

Not sitting.

Standing.

Feet spread a little wider than necessary. Like he was convincing his body to obey.

"Sir?" I said.

He turned slowly.

"Yeah… I'm just… dizzy."

He didn't smell much like alcohol. That was the first sign it wasn't about quantity.

"How long?"

He shrugged.

"I don't know. Since earlier."

"Have you been drinking?"

"A little."

Always a little.

He took one step. Didn't trust the second.

Reached out and leaned on the counter.

"Sit," I said.

He didn't protest.

He sat heavily.

"Water?"

He nodded.

Held the glass with both hands.

"Have you eaten?"

"Not much."

"Medication?"
"Yes."

That changed everything.

"Which?"
"I don't remember."

I didn't need to know.

"We're calling a doctor," I said.

He looked up sharply.

"No."
"Please."
"It's not a question," I replied.

Calmly.

He didn't get angry.

Didn't react.

"Okay," he said.

The ambulance came quickly.

They lifted him.

Asked questions.

Before leaving, he looked at me.

"Thank you," he said.

"If you'd left me… I don't know."

I nodded.

When they left, the lobby emptied again.

I thought how often balance isn't lost loudly. It's lost quietly. Inside a body that says "I'm fine" when it isn't. And at night, your job isn't to believe words. It's to see when the body says something else.

Night 50 – The Early Morning Apology

Alcohol has one good thing. It makes people honest. It also has a bad one. It makes them honest at the wrong time. It was just after four when the elevator opened and he stepped out.

Big smile. Too big for the hour. Wearing only a bathrobe. And slippers.

"Man," he said before reaching the desk,

"sorry about earlier."

"For which earlier?" I asked.

He stopped.

Thought.

"For everything," he said.

"If something happened."

That was suspicious.

"What happened?" I asked.

"I don't remember exactly," he replied.

"But I feel like something did."

He leaned in conspiratorially.

"I was a bit… relaxed."

A bit.

"Do you remember your room number?" I asked.

He smiled confidently.

"Of course."

Pressed the elevator button.

"Let's go."

"We're not going together," I said.

"Just tell me the number."

He looked at me like I'd asked for a complex equation.

"It's…
Wait…"

Looked at the ceiling. Then the floor. Then me.

"It definitely has four digits."

"It has three," I said.

"Oh! Right! Three!"

"Then it's… four–something."

I closed my eyes for half a second.

"Come on," I said.

"Let's take a walk."

On the floor, he walked slowly. Looked at every door like an old friend.

"Here!" he said suddenly.

I tried the card.

It didn't open.

"Not here," I said.

"Strange… I thought it was this one."

Two doors down.

It opened.

He stepped in. Looked around.

"Yeah… this is it."

"How can you tell?" I asked.

"From my pants," he said.

"They're there."

I smiled.

"Good night," I said.

"Good night…

And sorry."

"No problem.

We've seen worse."

He closed the door.

I went back down smiling.

I thought that in all these heavy nights, sometimes your job is simply to help someone find their room nd themselves at the same time.

And if in the morning they remember nothing, at least they'll wake up in the right bed.

Night 51 – The Nothing They Remembered

There's a kind of drunkenness that doesn't leave a headache. It leaves… questions.

It was just before five when they came down together.

Four of them.

Smiling.
Freshly washed.

Like they were coming from a spa, not a bar.

They lined up in front of the desk.

Perfect formation.

"Good morning," one said.

"We wanted to ask something."

That's never good.

"Of course," I replied.

They looked at each other. Silent consultation.

"So… last night… did something happen?"

I didn't laugh. That would scare them.

"What do you mean by 'something'?" I asked.

"Well, you know… something weird. Shouting. A fight.
Police.
Something like that."

Another nodded seriously.

"Yeah, because I remember being very calm."
"Which is suspicious."

"I remember being a DJ," the third said.
"But I don't remember music."

The fourth didn't speak.] Just looked at me suspiciously.

"And you?" I asked him.

"I only remember we lost a shoe. But we found it in the morning. On top of the fridge."

I paused.

Professional.

"No incident was logged," I said.

"No complaint.

No police.

No injuries."

They looked disappointed.

"So… nothing?" one asked.

"Nothing," I replied.

They stood silent.

"Strange," one said.

"We all woke up feeling like something happened."

"That's memory hangover," I said.

"The body remembers. The mind doesn't."

They laughed.

"Sorry if we caused trouble," the third said.

"Even if we don't know when."

"No problem," I replied.

"If you don't remember, it means we did our job well."

They left talking animatedly.

"Do you think we danced?"

"No, man, we don't dance."

"I had rhythm, though."

The lobby quieted.

I thought there are nights that leave no stories. Only question marks.

And on the night shift, sometimes, the biggest success is for guests to remember absolutely nothing.

Night 52 – The Naked Plan That Wasn't a Plan

Nakedness isn't always intention. Sometimes it's just bad planning.

It was just after four when the elevator opened.

And out came… him.

Naked.

Not dramatically.

Not provocatively.

Like someone who simply forgot something basic.

He stood in the middle of the lobby. Looked around. Looked at me.

"Good evening," he said.

It was the strangest "good evening" of my career.

I didn't shout. I didn't react sharply.

There's a second in moments like this when you decide whether it becomes a scene or a story.

"Good evening," I replied.

"How can I help you?"

He looked at himself. Like seeing himself for the first time.

"Uh… I think so."

"With what?" I asked.

He thought seriously.

"I can't find my room. And… as you can see… I'm not ready to be out here."

That was objectively true.

"One moment," I said.

I grabbed a towel from behind the desk. Held it out to him like an official document.

"Please."

He took it with relief.

"Thank you…

This wasn't the plan."

"What was the plan?" I asked.

He wrapped the towel. Took a breath.

"Bathroom.
Door closed. Then… confusion."

Classic.

"Which room?"

"It's… wait…"

Eyes closed.

"It has a view."

"That helps a lot," I said.

"Let's take a walk."

In the elevator, no one spoke.

On the floor, he studied the doors carefully.

Like he was choosing a life home.

"Here," he said finally.

Certain.

I opened it.

He stepped inside. Looked around.

"Yes… This is definitely my room."

"How can you tell?" I asked.

"From my pants," he said. "They're there."

I smiled.

"Good night," I said.

"Good night… And sorry."

"No problem. We've seen worse."

He closed the door.

Walking back, I thought something simple:

At night, some people lose their key. Some lose their room. And some… lose everything at once.

And your job isn't to laugh. It's to help them get dressed again— literally and metaphorically.

Night 53 – Check-out Without a Suitcase

A suitcase is one of those things you don't forget. Unless you've already forgotten everything else.

It was just after six when he came down to the lobby.

Calm.
Properly dressed.

Wearing a jacket, even.

Without a suitcase.

"Good morning," he said.

"Check-out, please."

"Of course," I replied.

"Do you have any luggage?"

He looked at me, confused.

"No."
"None?"
"No."

I looked behind him. Nothing.

"Did you leave it in the room?" I asked.

He thought.

"I don't think so.

I don't have much."

"How many?"

"One."

"And where is it?"

He looked at his hands. Then his jacket pockets. Like expecting it to appear.

"Now that you mention it…" he said.

"You're right."

No panic.

Revelation.

"Shall we go check?" I suggested.

"Yes, better."

On the floor, he walked ahead.

Not hurried.

Like it didn't matter.

I opened the door.

The room was empty.

Bed made.

Bathroom clean.

No suitcase.

He stood in the middle of the room.

"Strange," he said.

"I was sure I had one."

"Where did you come from last night?" I asked.

"From the airport."

"And how?"

"Taxi."
"With a suitcase?"

He thought very seriously.

"Now that I think about it…

Probably not."

"So you arrived without luggage?"

"Yes…
But with purpose."

"What purpose?"

He smiled.

"To leave in the morning."

I didn't laugh.

He meant it.

"Then everything's fine," I said.

"You're leaving the way you came."

"Exactly!" he said happily.

"So I didn't forget anything."

We went back down.

"Sorry for the trouble," he said.

"It was a good night, though."

"It shows," I replied.

He left whistling.

I stayed behind the desk thinking that some people travel light. Not just in luggage. But in memories. And at night, sometimes, the best check-out is the one with nothing left to forget.

CHAPTER 8

Staff vs. Reality

There are two hotels.

One is the one you see. The other is the one that works.

The first has brochures, photos, smiles, slogans. The second has tired people, shifts that don't end, and decisions made when no one is watching.

And somewhere in between, there's the staff.

What Corporate Thinks

On paper, everything is simple.

There are SOPs. There are manuals. There are online trainings with little boxes you tick.

"In case of a problem, follow the procedure."

In theory, everything works.

In practice, the procedure is asleep. And you're awake.

What Really Happens at 03:30

It's 03:30 a.m.

The groom might be done and sleeping. The assistant might be on another floor.

And you're alone.

The fire alarm goes off. Not a fire.

A faulty sensor.

But you still have to run. Check. Reassure.

No one will write in the report how fast your heart was beating.

When Staff Are People, Not Roles

Early in my career, I was bullied.

An old hand in the business. Bald, tall, from somewhere in the Peloponnese.

Instead of bringing new people in, he buried them.

Shouting.
Dismissal.
Fear.

That was "management" to him. I learned what I never wanted to become.

Greece and Abroad: Two Worlds

In Greece we have:

- receptionists with two, three languages
- *filotimo*
- experience

But often:

- low-level management
- no training
- "we've always done it this way"

Abroad I saw the opposite.

Average receptionists.

But trained managers.

Fire safety.
Health & safety.
Behavior.
Risk assessment.

And above all: respect.

The Loneliness of Responsibility

Night work comes with loneliness.

You finish in the morning. You want to sleep.

At noon you wake up a bit. Eat. Maybe go see the sea.

In the afternoon, sleep again.

Friends disappear. Your personal life shrinks.

Back then, I used to write "night philosophy" posts on Facebook. Unfiltered thoughts. Because there was no one else to hear them.

When You Cross Red Lines

After London, my red lines were crossed. I stopped tolerating certain things.

Respect.
Behaviour.
Professionalism.

When I came back to Greece and took over a big hotel, I wrote SOPs. I trained staff. I tried to pass on what I'd learned. But one incident went too far.

Rent-a-Car at Reception

It wasn't my idea. It was "how we work."

At reception—between check-in and check-out—there was always a voice:

"Rent a car?"

Not quietly.

Not discreetly.

Like a street vendor.

Guests looked. Some smiled awkwardly. Some got annoyed.

No one understood why it was happening there.

I reported it.

Once.
Twice.
Three times.

"Come on," they told me.

"That's how people make their money."

It wasn't their money.

It was the hotel's image.

I wrote a procedure.

I trained people.

Explained why it couldn't happen.

The next day, it was there again.

"Rent a car?"

Not out of malice. Out of habit.

I reported it again.

It escalated.

Not like an issue.

Like an annoyance.

That afternoon, the rent-a-car owner walked into my office.

He didn't sit.

"You're not selling my cars!" he shouted.

I didn't speak immediately.

"I don't work for you," I said.

"I work for the hotel."

The sentence landed heavy. Not because it was insulting. Because it was true. He shouted more. Accused.
Pointed.

I didn't answer.

That same night, I wrote a letter. Not angry. Clear.

The next day, I resigned.

I didn't step back.

Because red lines aren't theory.] They're the point where you stop shrinking yourself to fit.

When an Owner Loses Control

Another hotel. Another owner.

Staff parking on the main road.

I had warned them. Left notes on cars telling them not to park there. Updates. I'd informed all the HODs to inform their teams.

One day, the owner walked into my office.

Shouting.
Swearing.

"Get up from your chair, fatso, and go slash the employees' tires!"

My hands were shaking. I held onto the chair so I wouldn't raise a fist.

That's not character. That's abuse.

HR tried to keep me.

I didn't stay. There are things you don't negotiate.

What "Team" Really Means

A night manager isn't a lone hero. He's part of a team.

But a team needs:

- boundaries
- respect
- clear roles

You can't demand professionalism when you don't show it. And you can't demand loyalty when you don't protect people.

Why We Stay

And yet…

Despite all of it, we stayed.

Because when everything works, when the team locks in, when the guest leaves happy, you know you did something right.

Not because corporate told you. Because you felt it. And on the night shift, feeling is more real than any KPI.

There's an illusion in hotel work: that we're all a team. On paper, we are. In meetings, we are. In trainings, definitely. But at night, the team shrinks dangerously.

The ones who remain are the ones who can take it. And the ones who don't have a choice. Staff don't collide with the job. They collide with reality.

With hours that aren't written down. With decisions nobody explains. With responsibility that isn't paid more— but costs much more.

And that's where the cracks start.

Not dramatically.

Quietly.

There are people who enter the night shift thinking it's just another position. And leave understanding it's a role. A role with no stage.

No audience.

No applause.

And not everyone can take that.

In this chapter there are no "bad guys."

There are people:

- who broke early
- who learned wrong
- who shouted when they should have stayed quiet
- who stayed quiet when they should have spoken
- who left
- and who stayed a little longer than they could carry

Here you won't see guests. You'll see mirrors.

Because at some point in this job you stop asking: "Can I do it?"

You start asking: "Is it worth continuing to be like this?"

And the answer is never the same for everyone.

Night 54 – Bullying at the Beginning

At first you don't recognize it. You think that's just how the job is.

I was new. Not clueless. But new to that environment.

He was an old hand from the Peloponnese. Training me on hotel procedures.

Years in the job. And if needed, he'd done plenty of nights too. One of those who "knows everything" and reminds you constantly. He didn't always shout. That would've been easier.

He smiled.

"Leave it. I'll do it," he'd say.

"Don't get confused."

The first time, I felt relieved. The second, I felt embarrassed. The third, I understood. Every mistake grew. Every right thing went unnoticed.

"Who told you to do it like that?"

"No, no… this isn't a school."

In front of others. Always in front of others.

Not to correct me. To make me smaller.

I left my shift tired— not from work.

From pressure.

I started to doubt.

Not the position. Myself.

Until one night. Something went wrong.

Not serious. But enough.

He turned to me. Looked at me the way you look at someone you were waiting to fail.

"Told you," he said.

"You don't have it."

I didn't answer. I just looked at him.

And then I understood something that took me years to learn:

Workplace bullying doesn't start from strength.

It starts from fear.

Fear the other person will learn. Improve. That you won't be needed anymore. I didn't react that night.

Not yet.

But from that moment, I started taking notes.

Not about him.

About me.

About what I don't want to become when it's my turn to be "the senior one."

And that was the first real training I ever got on the night shift.

Night 55 – The Manager Who Shouted

She didn't shout at guests. That would be dangerous. She shouted at staff. That's always easier.

It was early morning shift change— when everyone is a little more tired and no one wants extra conversation. Something had gone wrong earlier. Not serious.

A billing mistake.

Fixable.

She walked into the office without knocking.

"Who did this?" she shouted.

She didn't ask. She accused.

I looked at the screen. I knew.

"Me," I said.

She snapped toward me.

"You?
Again you?"

The "again" was unnecessary. But necessary for her.

"You can't do everything wrong," she continued. "You're exposing us."

There were three people in the office. No one spoke.

"I already fixed it," I said.

"There's no issue."

That made her angrier.

"You don't decide if there's an issue!"

Her voice rose. Not from emotion. From habit.

I stayed calm. Not because I felt nothing. Because I'd learned.

"We can talk quietly," I said.

"We're working here."

She laughed, sarcastic.

"Here, I'm the one in charge."

That's where the conversation ended. Not out loud. Inside me.

"Not like this," I said.

Calm.
Clear.

She stopped. She didn't expect resistance. Especially not without shouting.

"Excuse me?" she said.

"We don't speak like that," I continued.

"If there's a problem, we solve it.

We don't shout."

For a few seconds, nothing moved.

Then she turned her back.

"We'll discuss it," she said.

Lower.

And walked out.

No one congratulated me.

No one smiled.

But when I was alone,

I felt something simple:

I hadn't won anything.

But I hadn't lost myself.

And in this job, that's always the first small victory.
And I told myself: I will never become that kind of
manager. Better to change professions.

Night 56 – Greece vs. Abroad

I understood it in the first week. Not from the work.
From the way people spoke. Abroad, a mistake isn't
shame. It's expected.

"What happened?"

"How do we fix it?"

"What do we learn?"

Three questions. In that order.

In Greece, the order changes.

"Who did it?"

"Why did they do it?"

"Who's to blame?"

And somewhere there, the conversation ends.

I worked nights abroad. First time alone. Real
responsibility.

I made a mistake.

Not small.

Not catastrophic.

But a mistake.

I said it immediately.

The duty manager came.

Looked.
Asked.

"Okay," he said.

"Let's fix it."

We fixed it.

"What do we keep?" he asked me after.

That confused me.

"What do you mean?"

"What do you take into next time?"

He didn't ask if I was scared. Didn't ask if I was ashamed. He asked if I learned.

Years later I came back to Greece. Same job. Same responsibility. Something went wrong.

I said it.

"How did this happen?"

"You weren't careful?"

"Didn't we tell you?"

The words weren't the same. The feeling was. They didn't want a solution. They wanted proof that someone was guilty.

Abroad, training comes before responsibility. In Greece, responsibility lands before training.

And then we wonder why people are afraid to decide. That's where I learned something no manual teaches:

The difference isn't the money. Or the systems.

It's whether you're allowed to learn without being made smaller. And for anyone working nights, that's the whole world.

Night 57 – The Trainings That Save You

Training doesn't show when everything goes well. It shows when something goes wrong and you don't panic.

I understood it on a night with nothing spectacular.

No fight.
No drunk guest.
No screaming phone.

Just a small mistake. The kind that happens every day.

Wrong key card. Wrong room. Two people in the same corridor who were never supposed to meet. My body reacted before my mind. Not from fear. From habit. I knew what to do. Not because I was smart. Because someone had shown me.

Step one.

Step two.

No improvisation.

It was over in five minutes.

No one understood anything.

No one got upset.

No one filed a complaint.

And that was what mattered.

I remembered the trainings abroad—the ones everyone hates. Fire drills at eight in the morning. Role play with scenarios that feel exaggerated.

"What do we do if…"

Back then we laughed.

Now I understood.

Because at night you don't have time to think. You only have time to remember.

In Greece, training is often just paper.

A signature.

A "you know this."

And then, when something happens, they wonder why no one knew what to do.

That night, I closed the situation without drama.

I sat behind the desk and felt something rare:

calm.

Not because nothing happened. Because if it did, I was ready. And then I understood:

Good training doesn't make you a better employee. It makes you a person who doesn't break when everything is hanging above them.

Night 58 – Self-Control

At night you learn to hold yourself back. Not because you're calm. Because if you let go, everything collapses.

It wasn't the first time I felt my blood rise. But it was the first time I understood how easy it would be to blow everything up.

After a hard incident, I came back for another night.

Not out of duty.

Out of need— to close it properly.

The lobby was quiet. Same as always. As if nothing had happened.

Someone laughed softly at the bar.

An elevator went up.

Life continued.

And I was still there.

I sat behind the desk and my hands felt heavy.

Not tired.

Full.

I thought about how many times I'd held back:

not to shout,
not to reply,
not to expose,
not to become what I had in front of me.

Self-control isn't weakness.

It's a choice.

It's knowing you can do damage— and not doing it.

And no one teaches you that.

You pay for it alone, night after night.

Before handing over the shift, I did the last round.

Corridors.
Doors closing.
Lights going out.
Everything in its place.

When I came back to the lobby, I looked at the clock. Time to leave.

Not angry.

Not victorious.

Just sure I hadn't let the night change me into someone I didn't recognize. And that— as quiet as it is— is always a win.

Night 59 – The Lesson

It didn't come like a revelation. It came quietly. The way the things that stay always come. The last night before leaving for Greece had no incident.

No phone call.
No fight.
No mistake to fix.

That was the hardest part.

I stayed behind the desk longer than necessary. Not because there was work. Because I wanted to remember.

The people who passed through. The ones who stayed. The ones who couldn't take it.

And the ones who learned to tolerate the wrong things.

I thought about everything this job taught me without ever saying it plainly:

That power shows in how you speak when you could shout. That "team" isn't a word— it's a daily action. That professionalism isn't a title— it's a boundary.

And above all:

No hotel is worth it if, for it to run, you have to make yourself smaller. I stood up. Did the final check.

Not out of obligation. Out of habit.

Handed over the shift. Passed the keys. Closed the systems.

No one said anything special.

And that was right.

As I walked out, I looked back for a moment. Not with nostalgia. With understanding.

I didn't regret it.

Because the lesson wasn't how to stay. It was how to leave properly.

And in a job that teaches you to keep everything standing, that might be the hardest thing you ever learn.

CHAPTER 9

The Shame Check-Out

Check-out is always more honest than check-in.

At night, everyone arrives with stories. In the morning, they leave with their body. And the body doesn't know how to lie.

The Hour No One Wants to Look at You

It's around six.

The sun starts slipping in through the lobby windows. Not quite light yet.

Revelation.

The first ones come down.

Sunglasses. Head lowered. Fast steps.

They don't say "good morning."

They say:

"Check-out."

Like they want it to end as quickly as possible.

The People Who Didn't Sleep Where They Were Supposed To

You recognize them immediately.

No suitcase. No plan.

Only that look of someone who spent the night somewhere they shouldn't have.

The man in front. The woman two steps behind. They don't talk to each other. They don't talk to me. They sign. Take the receipt. Leave.

And I remember who walked in with them last night.

They're hoping I don't.

Rooms Talk

After check-out comes silence.

And then… housekeeping.

Sheets thrown.
Towels on the floor.
Bottles.
Sometimes… blood.
Sometimes… pills.
Sometimes… nothing.

And that's the most worrying of all.

Rooms always tell the truth. They just don't tell it with words.

The "Gentlemen" of the Night

And then there are the ones who act relaxed.

"Morning, my friend!"

Now we're friends. Last night I was invisible. Today we're brothers.

"Everything okay?"

"Perfect."

No. It wasn't perfect. But now it's over.

The Look You Don't Forget

But sometimes…

check-out hurts.

A woman alone.

No makeup.

No armor.

She hands me the keycard.

Her hands tremble a little.

"Take care," I say.

She looks at me a second longer than she needs to.

She says nothing.

But inside that look is the whole night.

Why Morning Doesn't Forgive

Morning is ruthless.

The alcohol is gone. Excuses don't work. The lights are bright. And whatever you did at night… shows.

In the body.
In the eyes.
In the way you avoid other people's gaze.

The Night Manager Stays Until the End

When everyone leaves, I'm still here. An empty lobby. A chair I can finally sit in. The shift ends. But the night doesn't.

Because I know that in a few hours, it will all start again.

New people.

New stories.

Same decisions.

And I'll be here again.

Not to judge. To remember.

Night 60 – Sunglasses at 06:00

It was fifteen minutes to six when they walked into the lobby.

Not together. Never together.

He came first.

Sunglasses.

In winter.

In half-light.

He didn't look around. Went straight to the desk.

"Check-out," he said.

His voice was normal. His body wasn't.

"Good morning," I replied.

He didn't answer.

A few minutes later, she came down.

No sunglasses.

No makeup.

Eyes slightly swollen.

She stood a little further back.

Like she didn't want it to look like she knew him.

"Good morning," she said quietly.

"Good morning."

No one spoke.

The receipt printed. The paper sounded louder than it should have.

"Thank you," he said.

Without looking at me.

"Thank you," she said.

And looked at me a fraction longer.

Not asking for help.

Asking for confirmation that… yes. It was over.

They took their bags.

Not together.

The door closed behind them.

I stayed alone in the lobby, with sunrise slipping in carefully. I thought how unfairly people blame the night. It doesn't lie. It just lets the morning speak.

And in the morning, when sunglasses are worn without sun, you know someone is trying to hide something that can't be hidden anymore.

Night 61 – The Look That Never Lifted

He said nothing.

And that was the clearest message.

It was a little after six when he stood in front of the desk.

Alone.
No rush.
No luggage yet.

"Good morning," I said.

He nodded.

Not up.

Down.

"Check-out."

His voice was low. Not broken. Controlled.

I typed in the name. The system opened immediately.

I already knew what I'd see.

"Everything okay?" I asked out of habit.

It was the wrong question.

I knew it.

But sometimes you ask it not to get an answer, but to leave space.

He didn't reply.

He stared at the counter like he was counting scratches.

The receipt printed.

I slid it toward him.

"There you go."

He took it. Didn't look at it.

"Thank you," he said.

It was the first word he said while looking slightly higher.

Not into my eyes. At the level of my throat.

"Take care," I said.

He nodded again.

His head never lifted.

He turned and walked out.

His bags were already waiting by the door.

Like they knew.

I stayed behind the desk and thought how much a look can say when it refuses to meet another. It's not shame for what happened. It's shame for what he understood too late.

And at check-out, when the head never lifts, you know the night didn't leave questions.

It left answers.

Night 62 – Silence

Silence isn't always awkward.

Sometimes it's simply… agreement.

It was a little after six when they came down.

Together this time.

That alone was suspicious.

They stood in front of the desk.
Side by side.
Straight.
Like they'd rehearsed.

"Check-out," he said.

"Good morning," I replied.

"Good morning," she said.

And then… nothing.

No look.
No whisper.
Not even that tiny nod that says *you say it.*

I typed slowly.

Not on purpose.

But the system could feel the air.

The receipt took its time.

No one rushed it.

I watched from the corner of my eye.

They both stared ahead.

Not at each other.

Not at me.

Like two people who'd agreed that silence was the
best version of the story.

The receipt printed.

I pushed it toward them.

"There you go."

They took it together.

Their fingers touched for half a second.

Then pulled back immediately.

"Thank you," they said almost at the same time.

That was impressive.

They picked up their bags.

Not fast.

Not slow.

They paused at the door for a fraction of a second. Like they were waiting for something to be said.

Nothing was said.

The door closed.

I stayed alone in the lobby and smiled. Because in this job you learn something useful:

When two people say absolutely nothing, they've already said everything. And usually, it's better that way.

Night 63 – The Check-out That Looked Like a Movie

It was one of those mornings when the light enters the lobby like it knows more than you do.

Six-thirty.

Coffee had just been made.

The city was waking up, completely uninterested in what came before.

The door opened and three walked in.

Two in front.

One behind.

The first two walked normally.

The third… not so much.

No handcuffs. But he walked like someone who knew he didn't decide the route anymore.

Behind them: two police officers.

Not rushed. Not strict.

That relaxed seriousness that says:

It's over. We're just finishing it.

They stopped at the desk.

"Check-out," one of the first two said.

Normally.
As if two uniforms and a small story weren't part of the frame.

"Good morning," I replied.

I didn't ask anything.

No need.

I typed.

The system opened. The room was there. Charges clean.

"Everything okay?" I asked out of habit.

One officer smiled just slightly. The other looked at the floor.

"Everything… okay," the guest said.

With a pause in the middle of the sentence that separated *okay* from *not exactly*.

The receipt printed.

I slid it toward them.

"There you go."

The wrong person took it. Passed it to the right one.

They both looked at it without seeing it.

"Thank you," they said.

The third man said nothing. He just looked around. Like he was saying goodbye to a set.

"Take care," I said.

One of the officers nodded.

Not as a greeting. As recognition.

They turned to the door.

For one second, everyone froze.

Like a freeze frame.

Then they walked out.

The door closed.

The lobby stayed quiet.

I took a sip of coffee and thought:

Some check-outs have drama. Some have shame. Some have promises that will never be kept. And some…

Some are just a story that ended a little more officially than it began.

End credits.

No music.

And the best part?

For the hotel, it was just another quiet departure.

CHAPTER 10

The Survivors of Sunrise

Sunrise triumphant.

No music. No applause. never is Only light.

And light doesn't forgive.

The Hour Everything Goes Quiet

Just before six, the hotel changes again.

The corridors that were boiling earlier are now empty. The elevators move slowly. The lobby breathes. It's not night anymore. It's not day yet. It's that in-between hour that belongs only to us.

The Few Who Stay Standing

There aren't many survivors of sunrise.

It's:

- the night manager
- the first morning receptionist
- housekeeping starting quietly
- a taxi driver outside, engine running

We don't talk much. We don't need to.

A look is enough.

What Never Made It Into the Reports

There are things that were never written down.

Not because they shouldn't have been. Because they didn't fit a form.

You don't write:

- the racing heart before you open a door
- the weight of silence after an ambulance leaves
- the kind of exhaustion that makes you see life differently

You carry those with you.

Why We Keep Going

A lot of people asked me:

"Why did you do it for so many years?"

There isn't one answer.

Because:

- someone had to be there
- someone had to keep the balance
- someone had to say "no" when everyone else said "leave it"

And because sometimes—inside the chaos—you did something right.

The Loneliness That Stays

Night work changes you.

It cuts off friends. Shrinks circles. Expands thought.

It teaches you to carry things alone.

And that's a double-edged blade.

When You Step Outside and the World Wakes Up

I step outside.

The sun is a little higher. The world is going to work. Cafés are opening.

No one knows what happened a few hours ago.

And that's fine.

The night doesn't ask for recognition. It only asks that you endure it.

This Book

This book wasn't written to shock.

Or only to entertain.

It was written to tell stories that aren't told.

About people you don't see. About shifts that aren't applauded.

For everyone who kept something standing while the others slept.

The Final Thought

If you ask me what remained from all of this, I won't give you stories.

I'll give you this:

The night teaches you who you are when no one is watching.

And if you make it to sunrise, you've already won.

Night 64 – The End of the Night

After the last check-out, the hotel changes its face.

It's no longer a place of hospitality. It's a building breathing slowly.

Doors close softer. Footsteps sound clearer. Voices disappear.

I did the last round.

Not out of obligation. Out of habit I didn't want to erase too fast.

Lobby.
Elevators.
Corridors.

On every floor, the same quiet— with small differences. A forgotten light. A door open half an inch.

A Do Not Disturb sign that won't be disturbed again.

I came back down to the desk.

The morning shift was getting ready.

Coffee.
Paperwork.

The day was taking its place.

"Everything okay?" they asked.

"Everything okay," I said.

And this time, I meant it.

Nothing was left open. Not in the system. Not inside me.

I handed over the keys. Shut down the computer. Took off the badge.

Left it in the drawer.

Not ceremonially.

Simply.

When I stepped outside, the sun was already high.

Not for me. For the world.

I stood there for a second and thought:

The night never ends abruptly. It just… lets you go.

And if you did your job well, you leave quietly. No debt. No loose ends. Only stories you know you don't need to tell all of them.

Night 65 – The Lobby in the Light

Light changes everything.

Not because it reveals. Because it removes the mystery. The lobby in the morning doesn't look like the night lobby.

Same furniture. Same marble.

Different place.

The sun comes in through the windows without permission.

It doesn't ask what happened. It doesn't care.

I sat for a little longer.

Not behind the desk. Off to the side.

Like a guest.

I heard the sound of housekeeping carts. The first laugh of the morning shift. The automatic "good morning."

No one knew what came before.

And no one needed to.

The lobby in the light is innocent.

It doesn't keep secrets. It leaves everything to the night.

I looked around.

A lot had happened here.

And now… nothing.

That's the paradox of the job:

If you do everything right, it doesn't look like you did anything.

I stood up. Put on my jacket. Walked through the door.

For the first time in years, I left without looking back.

Not because it didn't matter.

Because it had closed.

And in the daylight I understood something simple:

The night doesn't follow you.

It leaves you where it taught you.

And then it gives you space to walk differently.

Night 66 – The Few Who Stay

Not many stay.

You see it in the lobby when everything is over.

Not in faces. In how they move.

The morning shift is in motion. Most guests are gone. The elevators go up and down empty.

And the few remain.

The elderly man who always sits in the same armchair.
No rush.
No questions.
He simply stays.

The woman with a coffee in her hand, staring out the window, not waiting for anyone.

The professional who opens their laptop before breakfast is even finished— like they need to prove the day has already started.

And the staff.

The ones guests don't notice. The ones who change shifts quietly. The ones who know what happened without discussing it.

The few who remain aren't the strongest.

They're the most ordinary.

The ones who can handle the transition.

From night to day. From tension to routine.

I watched them for a moment.

Not as guests. As people.

And I thought:

This job isn't for the moments when something happens.

It's for the moments when nothing happens and someone still has to be there.

The few who stay won't remember the night. And I won't remember them one by one.

But somehow, for a small piece of time, we shared the same space—after the end.

And that's always a quiet kind of company.

Night 67 – The Thought That Stayed

Nothing dramatic happened.

And that was right.

It was just a moment when I understood I didn't need another one.

The lobby was normal now.

Not bright.
Not dark.
Just… there.

Chairs in place. Coffee hot. Doors opening and closing like every morning.

No one knew it was my last night.

And there was no reason they should.

The night shift doesn't ask for witnesses. It asks for presence. I thought about all the nights that passed.

Not one by one.

All together.

The fears that didn't show.
The decisions made without applause.
The "no" said calmly.
The mistakes that never became news.

And then I understood something simple:

This job doesn't teach you how to control others.

It teaches you how to control yourself when no one
is watching.

I stood up.

Straightened my tie automatically.

Not out of habit.

Out of goodbye.

Before I left, I looked at the lobby one last time.

Not to remember.

To leave it.

Because the night never belongs to you.

It's only given to you for a while.

And then you hand it back.

And if you handed it back clean— without leaving
something behind that can't survive the light—
then you did your job.

That was all.

Not the end of a shift.

The end of a cycle.

And the last thought wasn't about what happened.

It was about what *didn't* happen because someone was there and kept the night standing.

And that, in the end, was everything.

For Those Who Stayed Awake

This book wasn't written to impress.

Or to explain.

Or to justify.

It was written because there are jobs that—if no one speaks of them—you start to believe they don't exist.

The night shift leaves no souvenirs.

No photos.

No applause.

Only people making decisions while everyone else sleeps. If you read these nights and recognized something of yourself, it's not an accident.

It doesn't matter if you ever worked in a hotel. It matters if you were ever alone with responsibility. If you kept something standing without anyone asking you to. If you said "no" when it would've been easier to say "it's fine."

If you left so you wouldn't lose something more important than a job.

This book is for you.

Not because you're a hero.

Because you did what had to be done—without an audience.

And in a world that screams, that's a rare kind of strength.

FINAL THOUGHT

When the night ends, there's nothing left to prove. Only to leave without leaving behind something that can't survive the light.

If this book kept you company for even one night, then it did its job.

Just like you did.

Good morning.

ACKNOWLEDGEMENTS

To those who worked nights and were never written into any book.

To those who held their boundaries when no one was watching.

And to a few people who allowed me to learn the job the right way — even when they didn't know they were doing it.